The last thing I remember is going to buy snacks for my road trip with Mitch. I don't know what happened after that, but I'm awake in a strange room. I think I'm in a hospital room, but something isn't right. I learn I'm now a prisoner, and these weirdly beautiful people can control my body.

I was pregnant when I left my home, and I'm learning, as a prisoner, that's no longer the case. They've taken everything from me, and now they plan to auction me off to the highest bidder.

Through the Gold
Copyright © 2024 Selina Rose
ISBN: 978-1-4874-4271-2
Cover art by Martine Jardin

Published by eXtasy Books Inc

Look for us online at:
www.eXtasybooks.com

THROUGH THE GOLD

BY

SELINA ROSE

CHAPTER ONE: PRODUCT

Before I even opened my eyes, I knew that I wasn't home. The air smelled too sterile — disinfectant, the scent of hospital-starched sheets, and some harsh lemon chemical. The unpleasant aroma clogged my throat and burned my eyes. Groaning, I tried to lift my hand to cover my nose, but my reach came short. *Way* too short.

With my tired eyes flying open, I squinted through my blurry vision, seeing that my hands were bound to the surface I lay on by thick, black restraints. *Dreaming. I must be dreaming*, I thought, but the chill in the air felt all too real.

I scanned my hand for the gold band on my finger — the symbol of Mitch's love and my anchor to reality.

Gone. My ring was *gone*.

I wiggled my feet with mounting horror, realizing that my ankles were bound, as well. I gave a sharp yelp, arched my back, and my eyes rolled in a desperate search for my unseen captor. The harsh light twinkled near my right foot, and I peered with confusion at the snug silver band around my ankle, resembling a bangle. My neck strained as I turned my head. I tugged at my restraints with all my might, which wasn't much in my weakened, groggy state, and I sobbed when I felt no give.

I wore the universal hospital gown, with my ass bare by the feel of it.

Horror movies started like this, and if I'd been a betting kind of girl, I'd have wagered that the grey, lifted, rectangle-shaped thing near my bed was covered in clean, sparkly, sharp objects on a flimsy paper mat, placed in order from the dullest to the most wickedly sharp. Some would be perfect for cutting small slivers of flesh as thin as tissue paper from the screaming patient. Others would be jagged and crafted for sawing through bone.

I sucked in air, whimpering, adrenaline clearing the last of the blur from my vision and causing a cold sweat to break on my brow. My head swam sickeningly as I lifted my upper body as much as my restraints would allow, noting the black bands on my abdomen and chest. Only my head was mobile. I tried in vain to fight the visions of my impending torture. My mind was painting a vivid picture of a masked man slicing one of my ears from my skull with surgical precision. My blood-soaked hair whipped wildly as I screamed and begged for mercy, bargaining and throwing prayers to any deity that could help a girl out.

My imagination was an asshole.

My heart rate spiked, thumping hard against my chest, and I sucked in air greedily and rapidly, feeling dizzy. My body quaked as I held in a wail of the purest of horror, not wanting to alert my captor that I was conscious. My shaking hands straining towards my belly. Towards my secret.

A hospital.

Maybe I was only in a hospital.

The possibility was like a valium to my soul.

A faint stinging sensation caught my attention, and I looked down, noting the—by the feel of it—rather large needle just below the crook of my elbow. My eyes trailed the tube attached that led to what I gathered had to be the IV pole, which beeped softly and slowly. The screen above glowed, and though I couldn't make out the digital readings, I assumed all was well. Those contraptions made a shrill fuss when someone was kicking the bucket, and though my heart felt like it would burst from my chest like a face-hugging alien, it was apparently still doing its job.

I was conscious and in one piece.

I bit my lip and wiggled my hips as much as I could manage, feeling comforted that I felt no wetness between my thighs, no padding. If I'd miscarried, I'd bleed, right? I'd ache. I was painfully new to the idea that a little person had taken up shop in my womb, but I knew enough to know that there would be some discomfort if I'd lost the mysterious little person that had attached itself to my innards.

There was no pain.

Just a persistent ringing in my ears and a chill spreading along my scalp. Blind terror merged with suicidal curiosity as I stared at the door.

Maybe we would be okay.

Maybe.

Mitch would be here soon and . . .

I tried to recall how I'd gotten here. Had I been in a car accident? A fall, perhaps? I shut my eyes, straining my brain to glean any recollection of how I'd gotten here.

I'd gone to pick up some junk food for the trip. I remembered the parking lot, the candy aisle, and walking to my car, plastic bags rustling against my side, and then . . .

Nothing.

I opened my eyes, sighing in frustration. I'd hit a brick wall. What the hell had happened to me? Blinking, I scanned my surroundings again, this time lingering on the details. Yes, this appeared to be a hospital room, but a *very* upscale hospital room. The door to the far right of the room gleamed a lacquered red, and the dark hardwood floors shined, reflecting the small, intricate chandelier above. A chest of drawers, though a boring grey, were clearly not cheap. The handles of the furniture curved elegantly, catching the harsh light and sparkling as if from within.

Crystal?

An equally boring shade of gray belonged to the chair nearby in the far-right corner, and I strained my neck, inspecting the bear-claw legs and the thick material, the plushness of the backing and seat. A small, gray leather pillow sat propped perfectly against its generously cushioned back. I'd guarantee the small throw alone would have been worth a large chunk of my paycheck.

A large oil painting hung in the center of the two fancy pieces, and my mouth dropped open as I studied the scene. I recoiled, horror and panic returning with gusto, lips peeling back from my teeth in distaste.

The art—a generous word for something so heinous—depicted a nude woman who lay screaming as little red devils danced around her writhing form with their mini pitchforks held high, their smiles stretching from ear to tiny ear. The unlucky beauty had long, cascading red hair, and within the tresses, I could see faces. *Screaming faces.*

No, this wasn't a maternity ward. And no, it wasn't the psych ward. The painting would have driven someone to suicide if they'd stared at it long enough, the artist having captured the damsel's mad look of torment perfectly.

My brain decided it was the perfect moment to recall a certain horror movie, and though Mitch had loved the film, during the scene where the dude's desperation had driven him to saw his own hand off, I'd struggled not to hurl into my popcorn. Now, nearly worked into hyperventilation, I waited for a disembodied voice to give me macabre instructions to complete if I wanted to earn my freedom.

I retched, but nothing came up. Clutching the sheets like they were anchors, I almost convinced myself that if I let go, I'd fall into the sky.

A click.

I didn't dare breathe as the door swung open, revealing a willowy, platinum-haired woman in a lab coat. The vision glided in like a heavenly apparition, high heels clicking on the spotless floor. Her impossibly ice-blue eyes demanded my undivided attention, and I wondered if the hue was courtesy of contacts. The effect had to be artificial, I decided, because one couldn't have eyes that pale, that luminescent.

Small glasses perched on the end of her tiny, upturned nose, and her full mouth was pursed in a look of calculation. Artfully braided hair snaked over her thin right shoulder, hanging nearly to her waist, catching the light and shining as if coated with a layer of black ice.

She walked like a supermodel.

I assumed she was a doctor or a nurse, given she held a clipboard and wore a stethoscope around her long, elegant neck, but I'd never seen anyone who's looks contrasted so wildly with their profession. She belonged on a catwalk, not a hospital.

"You're awake. Wonderful!" Her musical, breathy voice washed over me, soothing. She smiled, and her teeth were perfectly straight and blindingly white.

I said nothing but continued to stare. She was photoshop perfect, and I tried to recall anyone I'd seen, in magazines or on the tube, that was as beautiful as the woman in front of me was.

I couldn't.

She all but floated to my bedside, gazing down at me with those ethereal eyes, and I gasped, unable to look away. I wondered if I reached out to touch her, if she'd disappear — pixels scattered — the hologram of the world's most perfect female from an unseen projector interrupted.

"Let's take a peek, huh?"

I opened my mouth to ask a million questions, but the strangest thing happened — it clacked shut, my teeth loud in the quiet. What felt like an invisible fist pressed cruelly against my lower jaw, and I thrashed, my eyes feeling as if they'd bug out of my head.

Was this what a seizure felt like? Why wasn't she helping me?

A strange sensation crept over my scalp, the feeling not unlike dozens of tiny insects digging into the roots of my hair. It wasn't painful, but it was unbearable, and my hands twitched and jerked, trying to yank away the bindings so I could swat the crawling, burrowing things away. The woman watched with the same kindly curiosity while the feeling wiggled beneath my skull, and I whimpered.

She sighed and looked away, and the feeling of infestation skittered away as she made herself busy with a pen, scribbling away on her clipboard.

"Your thoughts are chaotic. Understandable," she mumbled to herself.

What kind of drugs had they given me?

Because people couldn't command ghost-bugs to descend upon your brain.

Her voice was husky, soothing, and I listened, feeling terrified of a repeat of whatever had just happened to me, my mind roiling with the unreality of it all, of her aloofness as I struggled to hold down my hysteria.

"I'm Doctor Anise, and I know you're terribly confused, but rest assured, you're in good health, and you're safe."

I said nothing, watching her eyes as she stared at my midsection.

"I'm sure you have many questions." She smiled. "And they'll be answered in due time, but for now, I need you to relax."

She grinned as she tucked the pen into the breast-pocket of her lab coat and reached out, her elegant hands coming towards my face. I jerked as her long, pianist fingers caressed my cheek in an almost maternal way, and though my muscles were tensed in fear, they relaxed as a liquid warmth spread through my jaw.

I could not resist, breathing deeply as the lovely smell of wild roses surrounded me. It wasn't a scent that could come in a bottle — it was as if she'd rolled in a pile of crushed petals. It was as if she was a rose herself, bursting with floral aroma after a summer rain.

Soft as down, the pads of her finger prodded my jaw as her lips pouted slightly and her head tilted quizzically.

"Now tell me, do you feel any discomfort? Cramping? Often the procedure is painless post-unburdening, but occasionally, my patients will feel . . . unsettled. Though I believe it's purely mental, we could elevate your . . ."

"What procedure?" My voice was a whisper, but I jerked my head away, my toes pointing in panic. "What procedure are you talking about?"

My breaths were fast now, too fast, and the swimming in my head increased, causing gorgeous Doctor Anise to tilt haphazardly in my vision.

"The pregnancy is no more, but trust me, it's far better this way." She turned, gliding away and turning with her hand on the doorknob, and gave me a magnificent smile. She winked, as if we'd just shared a special secret. An inside joke. "The flush in your cheeks is complimentary. It makes you look so very . . . young."

I went limp against the pillow, holding my breath, waiting for a small twinge of pain or a physical hollowness that would confirm the strange woman's claim that I was no longer carrying a child. I felt nothing.

I knew. I don't know how, but I did. Grief exploded in my chest, and I flexed my hands as numbness spread across my collar. The beginnings of a panic attack, I knew, not unfamiliar with the symptom.

She was still there, watching.

"Our healers are exceptional. You will experience no bleeding or hormonal shifts. It will be as if you were never with child. Anything you experience will be purely psychological." She sounded pleased. Proud. She wrinkled her dainty nose, making the skin around her eyes crinkle. "I never understood the inclination to reproduce among your kind. Stretch marks are unsightly. Your skin is so fragile."

They'd taken my baby.

The certainty that I would die here was secondary to the rage that began to heat within my belly. A belly that would not grow round with the symbol of the greatest love I'd ever known.

Mitch and I would not be married, and I would never, ever see him again. He would be beside himself with worry by now, and I wondered if he'd think I'd left him intentionally. That I'd panicked at the thought of taking our relationship to the next level. That, God forbid, there was someone else.

If he knew me like I thought he did, he'd know better. I wondered if he'd help search for my body. I wondered if there'd even be a body to search for after these people were done with me.

She studied me, her head tilted, pouty lips pursing in what I guessed was supposed to be sympathy. "If it's any consolation, our healers were certain you were to expel the fetus via natural selection in no less than three months. Your body simply wasn't prepared for reproduction, as there are structural abnormalities within your uterus. We saw no need to heal the defect. The correction is pointless in your situation and is not detrimental to your health outside of reproduction."

I gaped at her, tears rolling down my cheeks. Was she telling the truth? Would I ever get the chance to know?

"Who are you people?" I whispered, chin quivering.

She gave me a dazzling smile. "We aren't people, Kelly. You'd best remember that in the days ahead." She turned, managing to make opening the door look graceful, and slipped out.

I was twenty-five years old, and I was going to die.

There was only one way to convey my horror.

I screamed until my throat was swollen. I screamed until I spat out thin strings of saliva speckled with blood, staining the snowy sheets.

I had no idea what was to become of me, but I knew one thing—I was never going home again.

CHAPTER TWO: LIFE

M itch pinned me, grinning rakishly. "I've got a surprise for you."

"What's surprising is that you're not feeling queasy after eating all of that cake icing," I said in a purr.

He licked his lips, causing the place he'd eaten the dessert from to tingle.

"What can I say?" He rolled, pulling me on top of him. "I have a healthy appetite. I could go for another serving if you're up to it, birthday girl. Carbs don't scare me."

I laughed, propping an elbow on each side of his head. "Nope. You can't do that."

"Why not?" he asked innocently, his warm hands finding the bare small of my back.

"You can't tell me you've got a surprise for me and then distract me with *that body*." I pointedly glanced down at his chest. "That's cruel."

"Not my fault you have a short attention span. I think I should wait and reveal the surprise later tonight. You were, after all, born a minute shy of midnight."

"Hell, no, you don't." I collapsed on him, biting his shoulder. He laughed, trying to pry me away as I nibbled at the smooth flesh there, pinching the skin between my teeth just enough to cause him to yelp.

"Okay, *okay*," he said.

I stopped my assault, raising my head and scrunching my face in mock intimidation. "Surprise. Want. Now."

He pushed my body up by my shoulders, playfully tossing

me off his chest. I hit the mattress with a soft *oomph*, reaching to sock his shoulder lightly and contemplating a tickle assault.

Before I could poke his sides, his mop of curly black hair disappeared. He rooted around near the side of the bed, then rolled over onto his back, his eyes flickering briefly in my direction. He'd brought his discarded jeans with him, and digging into the pocket, he removed his hand, his fingers immediately closing into a tight fist, knuckles white.

He was nervous, I realized. That'd been trepidation I'd seen in his side-eye.

Lifting the firm body that I knew every curve and plane of, and then crawling over me, he planted one hand beside my head, his gaze level with mine. He brought his clenched fist between us.

"What're you holding?" I asked when he showed no signs of revealing the mystery thing he clutched. His fist shook ever-so-slightly, but I noticed. I noticed *everything* with Mitch.

With a little flourish, his fingers came undone, and pinched between his thumb and index, a delicate band of white gold glittered as it caught the noon light streaming from the window of our small, one-room house in the middle of nowhere.

The diamond in the center of the band held me suspended, and my jaw dropped, my hands coming up to cover my mouth.

He sighed, his breath smelling of buttercream.

"This is love, isn't it, Kels?" His eyes were shining, lips parted.

I took in his strong jaw with just the right amount of stubble — stubble that, this morning, had been a welcome texture in the crook of my neck. His roman nose twitched, a sure sign that Mitch was nervous, and it was a quirk I'd come to adore. Wide, hazel eyes bore into mine, hopeful, shining, wider than I'd ever seen them. His mouth, the lower lip fuller than the top and prone to pouting deliciously when I'd pissed him off, was swollen from my kisses. I reached up, sweeping his unruly curls off his smooth brow, and nodded.

"Yes, Mitch, this is love." I held my breath, sure that if I resumed breathing, the happiness combined with oxygen would make me explode.

"So . . . you will, then? I mean, it doesn't have to be soon. It doesn't even have to be this year, although that would be awesome, too. It's just whenever you're . . . I don't want to rush you, but we make so much sense and . . ."

He was rambling. Adorably rambling.

I cut him off with my mouth on his, bringing him down and pressing him against me.

"Yes, yes, yes." I breathed. "You know I will. You had to know that I will."

He pulled back, his right hand sliding warmly behind my neck. His other was planted beside my head, one finger lifting to lightly caress my cheek. I watched him as the trembling began, my chest constricting with a joy too big for my body, for this house, this universe.

He removed his right hand from my neck, his lightly calloused fingers trailing down my throat and slowly tracing my collarbone. My nipples hardened as I watched his eyes zone in on a bit of icing still on the tip of my left breast, the sugary confection nearly dry.

Mitch lowered his head, his tongue darting out and circling around the sensitive flesh. He withdrew too soon, and I sighed in dismay, only for him to return and pull the erect nub into his mouth, sucking it slowly clean. I cried out, my back arching, my hands diving into his curls, twisting there.

With the sweetness gone, he took my nipple between his teeth and bit down lightly, his hazel eyes lifting and burning into mine, hunger shining, reflecting my own. Mitch leaned back, lips parted, and almost reverently, sought my other breast with his left hand, his thumb making small circles around the peak. An emotion without a name passed over his face, and he shuddered.

His other hand trailed down my stomach, then farther still, and I bit down on my lip as he found the sensitive bundle of nerves that ached for his attention. His hand stilled, fingers putting firm pressure against my throbbing heat, but he didn't stroke in the way my every thought demanded.

I hadn't had enough of him earlier.

I would never get enough.

I shivered, my need expanding and tensing every muscle. My body thrummed with electricity only Mitch was capable of conjuring.

I was startled as he pushed my legs wide, his eyes never leaving mine. He scooted further back, the sheet bunching around his hips, watching me patiently. He wanted something from me, and I knew exactly what that something was.

He needed to hear me verbalize that I wanted him.

He tilted his head, waiting, his breath coming faster.

"Mitch," I whispered, unclenching the sheet with one hand and trailing my fingertips down my stomach. "I need you inside of me."

His eyes followed my hand greedily, and I slowed it purposefully, allowing one finger to swirl around my navel and eliciting a groan from the back of his throat.

I loved that sound.

I changed direction, my fingers skimming over my ribs, my breasts.

"Kelly." His deep voice sent shivers of pleasure down my spine. He was worshipful yet authoritative. Dipping his head, he sucked in a breath, rubbing his cheek against my knee. "Will you do something for me?"

"Anything," I breathed, squirming, near weeping with the glorious torture of waiting. My craving bid me to rush, even as I wished I could pause this moment and watch Mitch for hours with his desire making his eyes heavy. His pulse was visible in his throat. Beautiful. He was so goddamned beautiful.

He ran both hands down my inner thighs, pushing them impossibly wider, his finely muscled arms flexing as he dropped his head, his eyes taking in the part of me reserved for him alone.

"Touch yourself," he whispered.

I moaned, wasting no time. I was throbbing now. My body was a live wire as he watched me come undone. I bit down on my lip again, harder this time, tasting blood as I slipped two fingers between the silky folds and plunged them inside. I held his gaze in half challenge, half submission, but I was all his.

All his.

"Like this?" I whispered, my pace lazy, languid, in stark contrast to the overwhelming desperation I felt. This was maddening, and I relished it.

So did he.

His right hand closed around my wrist, pushing my fingers deeper.

"Yes." He sighed. "Just like that." His voice was low, gravelly, crackling as he began to lose control. I watched him fall apart beautifully, his forced calm shattering as I moaned.

His other hand closed around his hard length. I moaned again as he began to stroke himself. His firm abdominals were contracting as his pace quickened, and there was evidence of his arousal glistening on the tip of his hardness. He paused, removing his hand from my wrist and brushing the bead of moisture away from the head with his thumb. Leaning towards me, he brought his hand to my mouth. I parted my lips, allowed him to slip his thumb inside, and sucked hard.

That did it. Mitch closed the distance between us, pushing himself inside of my wetness. He plunged deep, throwing his head back as he pumped into me, my hips rising to meet him as he effectively pulled every fiber of my soul into the moment.

Before I'd known him, the weight on my shoulders had anchored me to earth, so much so that I imagined the ground would one day open and swallow me up, succumbing to the weight of a thousand bad memories. I would eventually bury myself, I thought. I'd dreamt there in static and black and white, not daring to hope. Not humoring myself with the possibility of happiness. I would always have dirt on my knees from my constant stumbling and mud on my brow from my falls.

As my body spasmed with release, I shot heavenward, my head in the clouds of his arms. His gasp as he called my name was the thin air beneath my feet as I rose higher and higher.

Mitch was where dreams manifested and took flight, and I never wanted to come back down.

We found out, more than an hour later and after finishing off the rest of the icing, that the ring fit perfectly.

CHAPTER THREE: ROAD TRIP

I submerged my hands into the warm, sudsy water, grimacing as my hand touched a gooey clump of mystery food. A swat on my rear made me jump, my hands instinctively rising out of the water, causing my face to get sprinkled with the gross dish-soup. I yelped, rounding to growl at my assailant.

"Let me have at that" — he nodded towards the dishes — "and you can take that sweet ass to the grocery and grab some snacks for the trip, birthday girl."

I blinked up at him, his whole face suggesting mischief.

"A trip? We're going on a trip, and I get to get fat on the way?"

"That's right."

I spun, facing him, my dripping hands rising to grip his forearms. He groaned, laughing.

"Tell me now." I bounced from foot to foot. "Tell me now and for how long."

"Two weeks. I told you I had plans for those saved vacation days, right? Susan's had a week's notice. She's cool with it."

"But where? Tell me!" I pressed myself against him, looking up into his amused, handsome face. "Pretty, pretty please?"

"I think maybe it should be a surprise."

"Like hell!" I bounced faster, this time in-place, like a jack-in-the-box on speed.

"What will you give me in return for disclosing this sensitive information?" His arms circled my waist as he nipped at my ear, his stubble tickling my skin, raising goosebumps.

"What *haven't* I given you this morning? Glutton."

"Here's the lowdown. A cabin. Georgia. And yes, it has a hot tub."

I squealed. Sure, to any other woman, the news might have made her day, but to me? This made my entire life. Mitch and I'd met two years ago at the same dead-end job at one of the three grocery stores in Langly, and as unromantic as it sounded, when our eyes met in aisle three right next to the expensive coffee that I couldn't afford but loved to sniff as I stocked it, something magical had happened.

Three months later, we'd moved in together.

We had so much in common it was scary. We both had a deep love of Chinese food, drunks for parents, and birth-marks in places where the sun didn't shine. He hated pop music, we both believed in Nessie, and we both had no clear plans for the future beyond surviving.

He endured my dark moods, and I weathered through his bouts of silence. We understood that both of us had scars, and we could both discuss them without pushing far enough to reopen them. We could each curl up with a book for hours comfortably, with the mutual understanding that it wasn't nice to interrupt one another's literary adventures, our legs curled together.

I loved him, and I knew he'd been scraping and saving for months. When I'd ask why, he'd insist he was making a nest egg to support us when we finally moved away and holed up on a beach somewhere in a garbage bag tent. Instead, he'd been saving for my engagement ring and painstakingly hoarding his vacation days so we could spend a romantic week in Georgia, sipping sweet tea and making love at our leisure.

He was silly. Wonderfully silly.

I squealed, kissing both of his cheeks.

"Oh my God, how could this birthday get any more

perfect?" My eyes misted, my lip trembling. He kissed my cheek and gently removed me from in front of the sink full of the dishes we'd neglected for a couple of days.

"Go. Candy, caffeine, and lots of it."

I practically skipped from the kitchen, heading to the bathroom to drag a brush through my tangle of sandy brown curls. I felt a slight twinge in my stomach. It was something that had frequently been happening over the past few weeks—not painful exactly, but odd and unfamiliar. I made my way quietly to the adjoined bedroom, rummaging in my purse for the small box I'd bought yesterday.

I had an irregular cycle and always had. I'd been told at a young age that the tilt of my uterus all but abolished any chance of pregnancy unless I opted for surgery. Glancing around, I was again reminded that I was in no way, shape, or form prepared to be a mother. Mitch and I had a long way to go before I even considered bringing another life into the world. And though I knew my suspicion was based purely on paranoia and what was most likely intense gas, I tore open the package and tip-toed into the bathroom to do my business.

I watched the test expectantly, knees bouncing, thinking that I'd buy *Reese Cups* at the grocery and thinking that this was just a precaution, a silly suspicion, something I needed to do before I boozed it up with my love in celebration.

My eyes widened on the two pink lines, and I nearly choked on my own saliva in disbelief. As my hands flew to my mouth to contain my shocked cry, the test skittered across the bathroom floor.

I grabbed the box, reading the instructions again. I yanked my phone from my purse, googling how common a false positive was. The site told me false positives were all but impossible, only negatives.

I pressed my hand to my forehead.

A mommy.

I was going to be a mommy.

18

I pulled myself together, numbly making my way from the bathroom. When Mitch inquired about my change of mood, I assured him it was only excitement and impatience. I escaped quickly, fake smile in place, and made a beeline for the front door. "I'm ready to roll. I can't wait," I said over my shoulder, but my head was spinning.

I'd stood in the aisle at the superstore for a full twenty minutes, staring at a box of snack cakes, my knees trembling. I imagined a million different scenarios. Everything from Mitch crying hysterically and calling the clinic to him shouting with glee and scooping me up in his arms like the fellas on *Hallmark* movies when their beloved reveals that she's expecting.

I was scared as hell.

I would tell him, I concluded, but after the trip. He'd been planning for months, and I knew he'd be watching my reactions to his gift, soaking up my pleasure, and I knew that dropping such earth-shaking news would consume his every thought just as it had mine the minute that I'd pissed on that *Dollar General* stick.

It was going to be hard, I knew, no matter what.

But it could also be magical.

I thought of those online college classes I'd toyed with the idea of taking, and I felt a spike of urgency I hadn't experienced before when thinking of furthering my education. A quickening need came over me to curl up with the computer and apply for financial aid with the long application I'd told myself I'd complete one day when the time was right.

The time was as right as it'd ever be.

I breathed through my panic, picturing a tiny bundle in my arms, little clenched fists flailing, and a wailing little pink rosebud of a mouth. It took me a moment to return to the present, and I realized was crying. Crying and laughing like a loon in the snack aisle.

"Oh, shit, get it together." I sniffed, fanning my cheeks with a box of chocolate-covered raisins as the last of the hysterical giggles bubbled out.

"Let me guess . . . a bad breakup?" A rich voice oozed behind me, far too close to the back of my head for comfort. My invisible boundary alarms shrilled, and I turned, swiping at my cheeks and staring up into one of the most distinguished, handsome faces I'd ever seen in Langly, Kentucky.

I noticed right away that as he smiled, his eyes were crinkling at the corners and twinkling merrily in the shopping center's lighting. He tilted his head to the side, his strong jaw clenching once as he winked. His black fitted tee clung to a body that was obviously very well cared for, and I instinctively took a step back. He seemed larger than life, and as his full lips peeled back to reveal a heart-stopping smile, I felt my feet carrying me back further. He had a dimple in one cheek, I noticed. A dimple that had no doubt dropped more panties than a *Josh Groban* concert.

Dark brown hair escaped the cap, curling along his forehead and brushing his ears. I glanced down at his crisp jeans and blue *Nikes*, then my eyes flicked warily back to his face. He looked wonderful in his casual attire, but it wasn't right. His dazzling smile was obviously confident, but his body language suggested discomfort. He stood like a man who belonged in something else. Army greens, maybe — no, a suit.

He looked at me like he was considering scooping me up and throwing me over his shoulder, and the hungry expression shot a warning jolt down my spine.

"Can I help you?" I near-whispered, years of customer service sending the words from my lips without thought.

"Help . . . *me*?" He grinned, shoving his hands into the pockets of his relaxed denim. "Actually, I thought that you seemed a bit . . . distraught. Can I help *you*?"

"No." I spat the word far too venomously, I knew, but I turned before I caught myself apologizing. Something about the guy unsettled me in a way I couldn't explain and didn't care to. Gorgeous as he was, his gaze burning into mine had felt invasive, an oily feel, and as the hair rose on the back of my neck, I walked away without looking back, grabbing a box of *Little Debbie's* on the way.

"Feel better, pretty lady," the stranger called, and I shivered at the tingle between my shoulder blades where I instinctively knew his gaze was settled.

"You're not helping, hot weirdo," I mumbled under my breath, walking briskly, suddenly eager to get home and hit the road so I could spend the entire trip my love was so eager to gift me and freaking out over my new preggo status.

As I'd checked out, I hadn't paid attention to my surroundings. I also had a scare after the cashier gave me my total, being unable to find my wallet in my mammoth of a bag, and I was nearly in a cursing fit when my hand closed over the plastic material. Fishing for my keys as I walked, and by some miracle, finding them within seconds and without the aid of my phone flashlight, exhaustion washed over me, and I wished I hadn't parked at the very ass-end of lane nine.

Pregnant ladies got tired easily, didn't they?

I tried not to cry again.

I'd opened the door of my car and slung my bag of junk toward the passenger side without a glance, certainly not expecting my goodies to make contact with a human. Especially not a very large, very smiley human. Mr. Snack Aisle struck serpent-quick with his large hand closing around the back of my head, fingers digging into my left ear painfully. The white cloth seemed to come to my mouth in slow motion, though I didn't have time to scream. I recalled biting him through the reeking, chemical-soaked rag, and his yowl as he struck me across the cheek with the back of his other hand. My head snapped backward as I was numbly wondering if he'd dislocated my jaw.

Then nothing.

Chapter Four: Pretty Devils

The memories left me quiet and vibrating with despair. When the door to my hospital cell opened again, I was unsurprised to see the grinning face of my abductor, though his face still stole what little air I'd managed to suck down in my horror. He was ruggedly handsome, and it was hard to believe someone so easy on the eyes abducted women in parking lots.

I flexed my jaw, surprised that I felt no pain from the backhand. No soreness. That couldn't be right. What was wrong with my body? An abortion and a smack hard enough to make me see stars, and I felt physically untouched.

"Pretty girl. I hear you came around."

"What is this?" I whispered. "Please . . . tell me why I'm here and what you're going to —"

"Shut up," he ordered. His smile was a contradiction — warm and amused. The casual clothing was gone and replaced by an expensive-looking grey suit with a blood-red tie. The combination was garish but suited him perfectly. The cap was gone, and it looked as if he'd taken pains with his hair. It lay back from his face, slick and glistening.

He clapped his hands together as his smile dampened only slightly. "You're alive and will remain as such. You'll only speak when spoken to. And you're to be sold to the highest bidder tomorrow. That's all you need to know."

"What? You're selling . . . me?"

"Correct."

"Mitch!" I called uselessly. My voice was shrill, panic

overcoming reason as I called his name uselessly. I struggled with my restraints and felt spittle on my chin as I bared my teeth, uncaring of the repercussions. If what I'd understood was correct, I would be sold into slavery and become a statistic. After I'd been used, I'd likely be murdered. My body might be discovered months, or even years later, in a dumpster, in a river, or maybe it would never be seen again. Maybe these people had a designated mass grave for people like me.

I imagined my drugged body sinking to the bottom of a pond, then crime scene investigators dragging me from the murky water with an algae-coated plastic bag tied tightly around my long-since decomposed face. Hair falling out in clumps. My fingerprints nibbled away by fish. Closed casket for sure.

I was a goner. I was doomed. I had lost my child before I could even fully absorb its presence, and the knowledge that I'd never feel the flutter of life in my belly again tore into my gut like a surgeon's blade.

I would not shut up.

I exploded.

"What have you done? What have you done to me? Let me go! Let. Me. Go!"

I would have him kill me before I would be sold to a rich deviant. I would curse him until he wrapped those large, menacing hands around my throat and squeezed until the capillaries in my eyes burst. I roared, sobbing and cursing my tormenter with gusto, and I wished that I'd given Mitch a sweeter, longer kiss goodbye.

"You fucking pervert." I spat, the fear draining out, a cold settling over me. A resolve to stop pleading. My thoughts were miserably clear, and they slowed and festered, anger filling my core. Wasting time on fanciful notions of freedom would only increase my chances of making it to tomorrow alive, to be raped, and God only knew what else in dark rooms with plump, evil businessmen. Maybe I'd be the starlet of underground snuff films. Maybe my screams would be someone's release in a dark basement room full of similar, illegal memorabilia.

In mere hours, I would be sold. No one would ever know what had befallen me. Mitch would go crazy with worry, then eventually, after my face had flashed on the local news and everyone who knew me had been questioned, he would accept that I was not coming back — that something terrible had befallen me.

And he'd be right.

This wasn't a sleazeball, underground operation. There would be no raid and no rescue. This man was a professional. This man would parade me and exploit me after he made me presentable. He had a doctor on call. I could only guess at the levels of security and the size of his staff.

Evil was a lucrative business.

"I told you to shut up," he said calmly, not a hint of annoyance on his face, but his hands opened, then closed. Opened, closed.

"Why don't you make me shut up?" I glared. Big words for a small girl. Big words that would hopefully push him over the edge and assist me with suicide.

His dark chocolate eyes glazed over as he pulled a pocket watch from inside of his suit. A muscle in his jaw twitched as he brought the timepiece to his mouth and fogged its surface over with his breath. He pulled a blood-red hanky from the same hidden, inner pocket of his blazer and proceeded to wipe the face of the expensive-looking fob gently.

"Coward." I spat, my throat feeling raw.

"I see you're a realist. But what you're trying isn't going to work." He sighed.

"That's just what a pussy would — "

In a second, he was on me, and I hadn't even seen him

move. I was assaulted with the scent of delicious smelling cologne only for a moment before my nostrils were pinched tightly closed. His other hand pressed roughly against my mouth, and all of my oxygen was quickly ripped away. I fought the urge to buck, to cry, and forced my body to go limp. I stared up into his eyes—beautiful, soulless eyes that a woman could get lost in easily, all while being aware that she was giving herself over to the devil, holding his gaze.

This was it—my only way out. Sorrow welled in my chest, and I blinked hard, feeling hot tears slide down my burning cheeks.

His hot breath fanned my cheeks as he panted, and he snarled like a beast. His rugged face was contorting and reddening. I only wished that I could laugh as I faded away to be with my son or daughter. The little spirit that had never had the chance to be flesh. I wished that I was capable of spitting in his face as I spiraled out into whatever waited, robbing him of the satisfaction of my terror.

Mitch would have been happy with my announcement of the baby, I decided, as the edges of my vision began to darken. My feet, however, would not be still as my oxygen-starved brain screamed for air, but I didn't resist as the room began to melt away, and my thoughts began to quiet.

I was giving in, and the place that I began to levitate to was warm and inviting. I tried to pretend I was in a bad dream and that when the vision of the man before me vanished, I would wake up in Mitch's arms, heart pounding, in sweat-soaked pajamas, but safe. Loved and safe.

When my tormentor released my nostrils and removed his hand from my mouth, I sucked in air greedily, my teeth aching from the pressure. I betrayed my resolve, tears spilling from the corners of my eyes as I coughed, my hands trying, and failing, to reach for my throat instinctively.

I watched him as he bolted away, stalking the length of the

room and muttering, with one hand raking through his dark hair, turning the neat style into something more savage. More suitable.

"You're going to live to see tomorrow. I do not damage my own merchandise. I leave that part up to my clients, and only after the sale is complete, you little *bitch.*"

I roared with rage, screeching insults through my tears, eliciting a cold grin from the bastard that had taken my life from me.

"I hand-picked you. I sat in your filth. I mingled with the degenerates. You are mine until tomorrow."

Then he was gone, and the loud slamming of the door jarred my guts.

I felt a twinge in my belly then, an ache, but I wasn't sure if it was physical or emotional.

I only hoped that my new owner would be ready for me.

They were going to find their purchase defective on so very many levels. Especially when it killed them.

I dozed, though I'd fought so hard not to let my eyes so much as slip closed, then groaned as I was awakened by a mousey-looking girl with dull brown hair swept into a severe bun. Her thin eyebrows lowered in what appeared to be dis-approval as she scanned me from head to toe. Her blue scrubs were so wrinkle-free that I imagined that she'd slipped into them outside of the door as they were pulled straight from the dryer and onto her rigid form by a maid.

"I'm to assist you to the restroom," she said, her voice a contrast to her plainness — rich and sultry. It was only then that I took notice of my nearly bursting bladder, and as I wig-gled what little my restraints would allow, I realized I was close to pissing the starched sheets. She nodded toward some-thing behind me.

"It's back there. First . . . I have something for you. It'll soothe the nerves." She smiled, but it didn't even come close to reaching her eyes. A syringe seemed to materialize out of thin air as she prodded the machine connected to my IV, clearly ignoring my hate-filled glare.

"I hope it's strong enough to immobilize me because, if not, I'm chewing your face off, Patty." She wore no identification, but she looked so very *Patty* to me.

She didn't respond. Instead, she set about injecting a gold, glowy substance into the tubing leading to my arm.

"That isn't very polite, Kelly Mayking. Do keep in mind that we are striving to keep this transition as smooth for you as it could possibly be. I understand your frustrations, but rest assured, they will cease to exist shortly." She smiled again as she trotted to the sharps disposal and flicked the needle inside. When she returned, she placed her forearms on the railing of the bed, cocking her head.

"That wasn't your run-of-the-mill-tranq, Miss Mayking. It's courtesy of the Faye, and for our safety, while we house the likes of you. It will blow that pissy attitude of yours to smithereens. You'll be shitting rainbows and pissing butterflies in the loo in a moment, as happy as a piggy in shit."

I didn't know what she meant by Faye. Was that some kind of code name for the psychos running this operation? Some type of black-market slang I hadn't heard of before? I wondered, vaguely, if the medicine would kill me, though she'd insisted it would make me happy. My demise was unlikely, considering they seemed to be taking pains to keep me breathing.

She'd said I'd be shitting butterflies.

Boy, was she ever right.

Whatever she'd given me was like liquid love as it traveled from my scalp to the very tips of my toes, causing a slow, lazy smile to stretch across my face. I giggled as I watched the good nurse undo my bindings and thought very seriously about petting her hair. She was lovely, really, if you could overlook the large nose and acne scars, and I wanted to pull her close and hug her so I could share a bit of the joy coursing through my veins.

I barely recalled the trip to the bathroom afterward, but I did remember pausing on my agreeable way back to my bed to ask Patty to engage me in a game of patty-cake. She snorted, saddening me for a second as she sneered a refusal. She didn't bother guiding me as I skipped the remaining couple of feet to the hospital bed and flounced on it like a fifteen-year-old girl who'd just had her first kiss. I even reached for the *Hello Kitty* phone that mysteriously appeared, marveling at its lightness as I held the pink earpiece to my head. *Britney Spears* blared out of the speaker, suggesting she was a slave for me, and I bobbed my head to the music.

I didn't like Britney's music, but this new, carefree Kelly did.

Patty watched me as I tracked the cartoon butterflies flitting around her head with delight. I bid her to sing along to the lyrics of the song, and she raised a brow, a small smile softening her face momentarily.

"Enjoy the high while you can, twit. I've got a feeling the betters will make mincemeat of you." And with a shake of her head, she left the room.

Mitch's face popped into my mind with the click of the door, but I pushed it away, sealing it in a pretty pink box in the cluttered back room of my mind. I closed my eyes, riding the wave of pleasure as my body thrummed with the beat of my heart, raising the tiny hairs on my arms.

I'd been kidnapped.

That didn't matter.

Nothing mattered with the gold liquid keeping me three-sheets-to-the-wind. Patty hadn't bothered strapping me back in, and as the room spun, I giddily guessed that there'd been no need. I wasn't going anywhere. I didn't want to. I felt as if I needed a seat belt, however, as the cosmos opened brilliantly above me. Stars shot across the neon sky, and a large, purple dragon rolled with a tiny moon as if it were a ball of yarn. It winked at me.

No. I decided. I didn't need anything.

Not if they gave me more medicine.

The rational part of myself watched in horror and profound disappointment, banging on the glass that separated her from control over my supplicant body.

They gave you an abortion.

I whimpered, shushing the voice and telling it to go away, but the nagging intruder that sounded much like myself chanted the macabre reminder over and over. The voice was making this so *not fun.*

Dead. Dead. Mitch didn't even know you were pregnant. They're going to sell you. They're going to sell you, and you'll be raped until you're dead. You're drugged. Drugged and docile. You're going to die. Dead! Dead! Dead! You have to move!"

"No," I pouted. "I can't."

Get your ass up! You're going to lay here and wait to be fucked to death? What would Mitch think of you then? This is not your father's cigarette burns, and this will not scar over. This is not the backroom of a party where you can pass out after you've chugged all the men out and hope one of the boys doesn't grope you while you sleep it off. There won't be a walk of shame. You're being sold by a monster and maybe even to someone who makes him look like Mr. Rogers, and you need to get up!

I obeyed, and even though the fuzzy feelings were bidding me to plop back down, I swung my legs over the side of the bed. I wiggled my toes, sighing.

A weapon. For the love of Christ, find a weapon, the voice urged, encouraging.

My high was fading quickly, and I moaned, smacking my

forehead with my palm over and over, each jar making my temples throb. I wanted to lie back down. I wanted to close my eyes and watch the beautiful colors exploding behind my eyelids. I wanted to be sucked into the cosmos in the ceiling and talk to the little green men that had peeked from around its corners, bidding me closer.

Defend yourself! You may not make it out of here alive, but you'll go out with what little dignity you have left. Maybe they'll run a train . . . a large line of wrinkly old men, the order with whom took their Viagra first —

"No!" I shook my head. "I can't. I can't."

You can!

I stood, my knees wobbling and threatening to give under my weight. The blue daisies that had sprouted in each corner of the room a few minutes prior wilted before my eyes and then disappeared.

"Okay." I nodded as the calm slipped away, replaced by horror and panic. My sanity returned with a vengeance, bowing me over, and I lost what little water the nurse had insisted I sip earlier as it spewed through my nose and mouth. With trembling fingers, my left hand reached for the tubing leading to my arm, and looking away, I stifled my cry as I tore the needle out of my flesh, along with the fine hairs there that the tape had grasped. I fumbled, tying my gown in the back, my gaze on the door, cold sweat popping to the surface of my skin and dripping down the back of my neck.

Good girl, I thought, back in control as I scanned the room wildly.

The metal tray that had been boosted near my bed earlier when I'd woken was gone, evidently whisked away by some unseen helper as I'd tripped harder than any flower child ever had. There was the IV pole, but as I gingerly plucked up the needle at the end of the tubing, I was disappointed to find it small and lacking for my plans.

I shuffled to the bathroom, holding my breath and hoping

that my feet sliding against the cold marble wasn't as loud outside of the doors as it was in my head. After scanning the bathroom and making a half-assed effort of ripping the metal pulleys from the toilet tank, I searched elsewhere.

And there it was, tucked in a corner I'd yet to inspect, to the left of the hospital bed. The most beautiful piece of manmade housekeeping gloriousness that I'd ever lay eyes on. I wondered if it'd been left accidentally but didn't question the gift from the gods as I hurried to pick it up, my vision still rocking, as if I were on a boat.

A broom.

And not just any broom.

This baby had a thick, stainless-steel handle.

I tip-toed, almost pitching onto my face as I wobbled, and made my way to the far wall beside the entrance. I crouched, waiting, bristles poking into my leg. After fifteen minutes or so, my calves were burning, and I breathed through my nose, willing myself not to hurl as the last, sweet fuzzies of my high disintegrated.

I hadn't known there were speakers in the room until the smooth, silky voice crooned out of them. I whipped my head around but couldn't find the source. His voice came from everywhere.

"That's the fastest I've ever seen anyone break through the gold. Impressive, Miss Mayking. I do have to tell you, with much regret, however, that unless you plan on sweeping your quarters, the broom goes back to the corner. If you disobey, the room will fill with a vapor that will render you unconscious for several hours, and upon waking, you'll experience the worst nausea of your life."

"Fat chance." My voice trembled, but I forced a laugh. "I'll stay right here, and as soon as that door opens, someone's getting a migraine."

"You think I bluff."

"Yes."

"Very well."

As the room filled with grey smoke, I held onto the broom, as if I could sweep the noxious gas away. As if I could wiggle my nose and catch a ride out of this hellhole.

The last thing I remembered was the floor coming curiously closer to my face.

CHAPTER FIVE: MAKEOVER

I woke again to complete disorientation and vomit spewing from what felt like every hole in my head. Hot water pounded my back mercilessly, and I moaned for whoever was in control of the stream to cool the temperature. On my hands and knees, naked, I retched, collapsing several times into the mess I'd made.

"Sit upright," a clipped, female voice commanded.

"Please." I hated myself for the whining tone, the desperation I heard there. "I'm so sick. The water's too warm. It's making it worse." Water dripped from my nose and chin, and I shivered, despite the heat.

"Cold water isn't going to wash the bile from your hair."

"God, just turn it down a little, you *bitch*."

There was chuckling behind me, and then, blessedly, a river of lukewarm liquid ran down my shoulders. I kept my eyes squeezed shut as I lifted my body, reluctant to open my eyes to any type of light while my head pounded like an African drum.

"Sit on your backside and tilt your head back, please."

"Please? As if I have a choice?" But I did as the mystery woman asked, thankful that the water disguised the tears rolling down my cheeks.

"I'm going to wash your hair now. You've made quite the mess of yourself."

"Up yours." I croaked, knowing that I was in no position to be snarky but unable to stop myself. I would not go about my strange grooming politely.

There was tsking behind me. "You've quite the knot on your forehead. That will need fixed before tonight. It resembles a baseball, if you care to know."

"I don't."

"Well, now you do, anyway."

I had no idea how much time had passed, but from what the mystery salon lady had said, I'd slept away my one remaining night as a free woman. Fantastic.

A sickeningly sweet, floral fragrance surrounded me, and I shuddered as fingers worked through my hair. When another pair of hands other than hers joined, scrubbing my back, I whipped my head around, losing strands from my soaked tresses in the process. The women were twins, I noticed as I wiped the water from my eyes, and my stomach was still doing backflips. Short, blonde bobs, frosted to perfection, were beginning to frizz with the steam of my bath. They both had identical upturned noses, big, grey eyes, and a beauty mark just below their left nostrils. They were ridiculously tiny, but lovely in their wispy frailty, and I wondered if I could take them both.

As my stomach lurched again, I decided that wasn't in the cards.

The tub was black granite, and I watched as one of the twins placed the detachable shower head back in the gleaming, steel handle to my right. I heard the water draining, pieces of my stomach swirling with it, and then the loud thrum of liquid behind me as Twin One turned on the faucet.

Twin One resumed scrubbing my scalp, and I went limp, all notions of escaping as naked as the day I was born leaving with the resuming of my pounding headache.

I was given more happy juice later, though I didn't make it easy, going down kicking and screaming as two large, rather violent-looking males pinned and strapped me to the bed before Nurse *Patty Tightbun* injected me with pure joy.

Afterward, I watched with amusement as I was given a lovely pedicure and manicure and cried like an infant as every hair on my freshly scrubbed body was ripped away unceremoniously by Twin One and Twin Two via wax strips. My long, chestnut hair was dried, straightened, and curled at the ends, and my addled brain somehow concluded that I was being prepped for prom.

I asked for my corsage repeatedly as Twin One plucked my brows and Twin Two fussed over my misbehaving hair, but neither would humor me. When a tall, dark-haired woman with long, stick-straight hair and a form-fitting pantsuit came in to yell at the twins about which dress she preferred out of the rack rolled in to work me into, much to my delight, a purple unicorn joined her. As I giggled and tried to feed it grass that had sprouted at my feet, the tall woman rolled her eyes.

"Must they fuck them up so completely before wardrobe?"

The twins tittered, earning a frown from the unicorn lady.

After I was dressed, I was strapped and left again to hallucinate wildly, ignoring the ever-building, nagging lady that sounded so much like myself that kept ordering me to snap out of it. I didn't resist as the two large men returned and unstrapped me, sitting me up, and even smiled at them as one of them slipped pretty, black stilettos on my feet. I stood, with assistance, in my criminally tight red cocktail dress and gasped as one of the men copped a feel of my ass through the thin silk.

"That wasn't very polite." I pouted, trying to focus on the offender's dark-skinned, pock-marked face as the room breathed and rained glitter around us.

"Ain't nothin' polite about what's comin' to ya, neither." He sneered.

"The boss will gut ya." The other, less scarred man with shaggy blond hair warned the other.

"She ain't got time to cry." Scarred dude spat. "You'd do

the same if you wussunt such a pussy."

"Naw, man." Shaggy shook his head. "I might be workin' for the devil, but I don't gotta go that low."

They guided me down so many hallways that I lost count. Chandeliers glittered invitingly, and thick plush carpet snagged my heels, making me feel off balance. I clutched the man with shaggy blond hair since he seemed kinder, and the nagging voice in the back of my head rose to a crescendo.

Showtime! For fuck sake, kick them in the balls! Bite! Punch! Scratch! You're being led to auction, and you're just going to hum the Aladdin song?

It was only then I realized what I'd been humming, but it seemed so fitting. This *was* a whole new world, right? Sweat began to trickle between my shoulder blades as the panicked voice became louder. Distressed, my lips quivered.

Hello-o-o-o! I'm your rational side, held captive by hard drugs, and I'm telling you, do something!

My legs buckled as if they had a mind of their own, while my feet began to drag. The two muscled cronies pulled me along, not missing a beat, and I began to whimper.

"I wanna go home," I whined. "Something's wrong, and I want to go home."

"Is that so, doll?" Scars asked. "Well, shit, me, too, but we all gotta hustle now, don't we? Don't worry, precious. You'll be going home soon. A new, shiny home with high-level security and toilets you could eat your caviar off of."

"You're such a jerk, man." Shaggy sighed, his disgust evident.

"And you"—Scars smiled, eyes on his friend and his fingers biting painfully into my arm—"ain't got a fun bone in your big ol' body."

The blond man snorted as they came to a stop, and I looked up, sure that I would've toppled forward or broken an ankle by now in my large heels without my escorts' assistance. My high was evaporating like dew in the sun, and I grit my teeth, silently rejoicing the rising clarity, as the weaker part of me missed the surrender of the high.

I turned my head slowly, and to my surprise, women were lined on both sides of me, each guarded by two men, the goons' elbows all but brushing. I tried to control my breathing as I scanned the faces that I could glimpse in between the bodyguards. Some of the women's faces were blank, some of their lips were stretched in elated grins, and some wept quietly.

All of them, though, had the same heavy lids, the same pink flush to their cheeks, and all of them were uncommonly beautiful and dressed like the world's most expensive whores. Each of us, I noted, were strategically placed in front of separate doors on the far wall. I tried to do a count of the gold, curving handles attached to heavy, lacquered oak with my sluggish brain since I couldn't count the women with all the large, scrub-wearing males clogging the otherwise wide hallway. I lost count as Scars cupped my ass again. I forced myself to pout as I had while blitzed, though it killed my soul. I really wanted to drop to my knees and punch his balls until my fists chafed.

Let them think I was higher than Everest.

I counted the doors again.

Twelve.

I scanned the hall on both sides, looking past a combination of *Cinderella* gowns and dresses that might as well have been crafted from saran wrap. It appeared that there were trios in front of each door, and the women were all dwarfed by hired muscle on each side.

My heart squeezed.

I flicked my gaze over to blond guy, watching as he whispered seemingly to himself, then he nodded, his finger pressed against something in his ear canal. I looked to my left, then my right, trying to ignore the beautiful, ebony woman with short-cropped hair and uncommon blue eyes as she talked in gibberish to something I couldn't see. She paused, eyes widening, and laughed uproariously, slapping her knee.

The rest of the guards were nodding as well, the one to my right mouthing *affirmative*

Almost showtime.

God, how I wished they'd at least placed me in shoes more fitting for a suicide mission.

I dropped my head, giggling, forcing my body to relax.

"Are you my chaperones for the dance? My father is so overprotective. Not fair." I hoped the whining tone was convincing. I wanted to barf on the red silk vacuumed to my body.

"They're so precious when they're blasted off their sweet petunia's," Scars muttered, scratching his nose and sniffing. I noticed a white substance in his left nostril. Charming. "Wish he'd hurry this shit along already. They said it'd be about ten minutes."

I looked behind me, startled by my own reflection in a large teardrop-shaped mirror with curling, silver designs around the edges.

My long chestnut hair spilled down over my pale shoulder, the V-shape of the dress dipping dangerously low to the small of my back. My brows were now sharply arched, penciled the same shade of my hair. My makeup, surprisingly, was minimal and applied to enhance rather than change my look. My already generous lips were glossed a luminescent pink, making them appear fuller. And my thin, slightly crooked nose, which had said *hello* to a baseball in fifth grade, was powdered, with one stray freckle on the left side of the bridge still plainly visible. My high cheekbones stood out with a dust of blush, and my wide, cobalt-blue eyes were lined to accentuate the strange color that Mitch had adored.

I didn't recognize the woman staring back at me, and all the makeup and glitz in the world couldn't disguise the stark look of terror that parted my lips and made my eyes appear too large for my face.

My chin trembled, and I looked away, closing my eyes for just a moment and taking a deep breath. Composing myself, I looked coyly over my shoulder again, but this time, at Scars, flashing him what I hoped would pass as a flirtatious smile.

"You must be my date, handsome." I batted my eyelashes at him stupidly.

He grinned, revealing a chipped front tooth, and his beefy hand tightened on my shoulder. I parted my lips, hoping that my eyes shined with what Scars would perceive as drunken desire, bringing my mouth close to those calloused, sausage fingers.

I placed one butterfly kiss on his thumb, staring up into his pig-eyes as they widened with shock under thick, caterpillar brows, then I moved on to the tip of his index. Sighing, fanning hot breath over the webbing of his disgusting paw, I nibbled my lower lip. I glanced down, noticing his drawstring scrubs were pitching a rather pitiful tent, and my stomach flipped, bile threatening to rise in the back of my throat.

Boldly and with much protest from my stomach, I licked the tip of the finger he no doubt liked to wag at terrified women who'd been ripped from their lives and brought to a mansion of horrors. Scars groaned, his grin transforming into an *O* of surprise. His eyes dulled, glazing over with obvious lust.

Perfect.

The hand he gripped my shoulder with loosened as I let the disgusting digit slide between my lips—which tasted vaguely of cheese and something else I'd rather not try to identify. He moaned low, his eyes slipping shut for just a moment, and his grip freeing me entirely.

I didn't wait.

I turned my head, angling my neck sharply, the middle

joint of the vile flesh between my molars and the tip of his dirty fingernail stinging my jaw, and bit down harder than I'd ever bitten anything in my entire life. I shook my head like a rabid dog, gristle and bone crackling, metallic blood gushing hotly into my mouth. Scars jerked his hand away with a pain-filled bellow.

I felt horror beyond anything I'd ever experienced as I re-alized half of his finger was still in my mouth, detached. I spat it out, watching in stupefied disgust as it bounced once on the carpet near Scars' large feet. Blond Goon's hand loosened in surprise on my right shoulder, and I spared him a quick look. He stared at his screaming friend with a look of comical con-fusion.

"Burt?" he peeped, brow furrowed as his friend roared, blood shooting in a long arc over my head.

I didn't pause to wipe the gore from my lips, which con-tained God-only-knew what kind of pathogens.

I bolted.

And made it perhaps ten feet, clumsily evading big hands that shot out like pistons as I awkwardly jogged past the other staff and victims on the thin stems of my stilettos, the silver band around my ankle starting to feel unnaturally warm.

She appeared in front of me — the stunning doctor who'd so coldly delivered the news that she'd murdered my unborn child. She was wearing a gown that appeared to be woven from intricate spider webs that pooled on the floor behind her. Tiny diamonds dripped in a V over the pale backs of her lovely hands — which she clenched over and over.

The doctor's beatific smile was gone.

Large, icecap eyes drilled into mine, unnaturally invasive, and I tried to focus on her lovely pale hair instead, piled into a glamorous updo upon her head, a few silken tendrils escap-ing. My eyes slid back to hers, the effort of trying to look away, making them feel as if they'd pop out of my head.

One coy smile from her enchantress' mouth, and I was on my knees, the soft carpet cushioning the insane force with which I'd fallen. My head was jerked upwards to accommodate her gaze by whatever wicked force she commanded, and the tendons in my neck strained.

I was being burned alive from the inside, lava coated my lungs and stomach, charred through my intestines, and shot flames into my throat. A high keening sound was coming from somewhere, the sound so full of agony that I wished I could cover my ears, but my arms were glued to my sides, my fingers splayed so widely I half-expected them to break.

As my brain seemed to swell, I realized that the pathetic, piercing cries I'd heard were my own, but they were cruelly cut off as my windpipe was squeezed shut by invisible hands. Something wet was leaking onto my face, something warm, but I couldn't bat my eyes. My vision tinted red.

I was dying.

Though complaining, when she spoke, she sounded pleased. "Being demoted to veterinarian of the damned has been the most torturous experience of my life, but it's small, quiet moments like these that remind me that even the lowest of positions can be rewarding." She smiled ferociously, daintily lifting her gown and making her way toward me. The squeezing of my windpipe increased, and I felt horrifyingly close to emptying my bladder while my head still, by whatever dark power this possessed woman wielded, arched painfully back. As my vision started to darken into what I prayed was unconsciousness, a type of sick glee filled me, a devilish thrill of success at escaping my new life as an animated blow-up doll, and I wanted to thank her.

I would have kissed her feet if I could have seen them or moved a muscle.

Perhaps I was mental.

But God, I didn't care.

I would be on my way out to whatever waited beyond. I wondered if it'd be better or worse. I also wondered if I'd shit here in the hallway — that happened after death, right?

I hoped that she'd step in it. I hoped the smell dampened her pleasure.

Then the pressure was gone, and I was gasping, choking on the oxygen I sucked down, my mouth wide. I collapsed onto the thick red carpet, the black veil of oblivion receding and affording me a view of the doc's beautiful heels.

The scent of roses clogged my throat, overwhelming as my lungs starved for fresh, clean oxygen, and I rolled onto my back, staring up at the ceiling.

"You'll go back to your escorts, and whenever that door opens, if there is any misconduct on your part, I will take you to a special room here at the facility. I will chain you there, and I will leave you for the male staff as a free-to-use tool for release. Does that sound enjoyable, Kelly?" she asked sweetly, her nostrils flaring and betraying her tone.

I felt my face crumple and hated myself for it. I turned my head, refusing to answer, remembering how Scars had cupped my ass. After biting off part of his handy-dandy girl-friend, I could only guess at the horrors I'd endure if I were chained, helpless, and unprotected.

Some things are worse than death. Anyone who even half-ass followed the news knew that.

"I asked you a question, Kelly." Her voice, dripping honey, was compelling. A grunt grasped my attention, and some-thing sharp was stabbed into my thigh, accompanied by an oily male chuckle. More of the good stuff made its way into my limbs and curled in my belly for a moment before giddily flooding my brain with artificial delight. I weakly rolled my head to my right, my eyes finding the doctor's, and I sighed, grasping to my reason with all of my might before it floated away on a river of gold.

"So above us, and yet, you can't manage us without drugs," I whispered.

A sharp stab in my lower belly, just above my pelvis, and I cried out.

"Will you behave or not, Kelly Mayking?" Her voice held the hint of a tremble, and her eyes seemed to catch fire. She tapped her foot impatiently, eyes flickering towards the doors with what looked like nervousness.

She was done fucking around.

Another stab, and I groaned like a dying walrus, my nails digging into the carpet and breaking. A small part of me wondered if the wrecked manicure would knock my sale price down.

"Yes," I moaned. "Yes!"

The pain instantly subsided, and I swatted angrily at the tears rolling down my temples. My shaky hand came away crimson.

Blood.

I'd been crying blood.

I made a small sound of defeat as I was dragged to my feet by one of the lackeys behind me, biting my tongue in the process and staring at my fingers as if they'd turned to snakes.

The doctor snapped her fingers, and a small, petite redhead with kind green eyes and nervous hands crept out from behind her, the girl's shoulders hunched as she worried her bottom lip with her teeth. The doctor turned her head, the light catching her platinum hair, causing it to glow like a halo.

She addressed the girl. "Her mascara is ruined. Fix it."

The girl, who looked to be not a day over seventeen, bobbed her head and removed a small knapsack from her shoulder. With small, jerky movements, she rooted around the inside of the bag. She plucked a small, damp pad from a tiny plastic package and began to wash around my eyes. As I hiccupped and attempted to keep the waterworks at bay, I saw her mouth soften in unmistakable sympathy. I wondered if she was here by choice, and when her hand paused for a second, I met her eyes, reading my answer there.

I imagined that sympathy wasn't tolerated here and wondered how long she'd had this job. However long, I'd bet she wouldn't last the year.

So all of us weren't auction material, but we were prisoners, just the same. The girl's circumstances, I suspected, could rival and even surpass my own if what I'd witnessed so far was any indication. My makeup was reapplied with the redhead's speedy, nervous fingers, and her eyes were flickering around her every minute or so in obvious fear. After applying a fresh layer of powder over my cheeks and nose, she nodded, her lips a grim line.

I was dragged back into position by the shaggy blond, and he leaned in close enough that his hair brushed my cheek as we took our place in line.

"Don't go bitin' me, or I'll snap your damned neck."

I stiffened, and I heard him grunt, his fingers loosening just a fraction on my arm.

"Didn't like the way he was treatin' ya, though. 'Tween you and me, that fucker deserved it. Ain't right to treat no girl like that. I got sisters. That shit burns me up."

I ignored him. Too much wind had been knocked out of my sails to mock his custom morals, and the injection was speedily going to work. I wondered what the blond's sisters believed he did for a living. The ragged ends of my acrylic nails bit into my palms, and I shut my eyes, increasing the pressure, attempting to make my mind blank with the sting.

Shaggy at my ear again, his breath tickling the side of my throat. "Don't talk to 'em like that. The doc . . . the ones you'll be sold to are like her, and in case you ain't noticed, they're special. Special, as in, they'll cripple you and poke you with a stick for a hundred years if you piss 'em off. Keep your head down and do what they say if you want to keep your limbs. Thirty seconds left until that door opens. Godspeed, girl, but he ain't following you to where you're going."

Chapter Six: Showtime

I could have never imagined what lay beyond, not in a million years.

Shaggy's frisbee-sized hand on the small of my back gave me a gentle push, and as soon as I stepped over the threshold into the softly lit, carnivorous room, the air thickened as if lightning were ready to strike me. The pregnant silence made the pounding of my heart so audible that I wondered if Shaggy could hear it. For a big guy, he stepped lightly, and the previous raggedness of his breath hushed in what struck me as reverence.

I staggered back. What I could only describe as raw, alien power was raising every hair on my body. Shaggy's hand, more insistently, pushed me forward, and I moved as if underwater. The strange pressure that seemed to vibrate my bones and pulsated on my skin like the reverberations of a giant heart were nearly unbearable. Like nails on a chalkboard, if the screeching was in your blood instead of your ears.

"Oh, God, help me," I whispered, the unreality of it all crashing on me.

What the hell is this?

The brain, I learned then, can only process so much of what defies explanation before it begins to shut down. A lifetime of mental conditioning, of believing in nothing beyond my bubble of humanity, was crushed beneath the heel of a Cinderella slipper and then ground to dust by the row of unearthly, beautiful creatures that came into focus as my clumsy feet carried me towards the front of the stage.

I squinted under the spotlights above, but there was no mistaking the men in front of me for human. I wanted to look away, to squeeze my eyes shut and curl into a ball on the glossy marble below me, but I stared at each of them, my gaze finding each set of ice-chip eyes just as beautiful and emotionless as the next.

They were impossible. Nothing so deliriously stunning should exist.

I heard the other women gasping on either side of me, and then the power was pressing down upon my head and my quaking shoulders as an unseen presence pushed me to my knees. The sharp crack of bone against the marble as my knees made contact with the surface below was almost as loud as the blood pounding in my ears. The band around my ankle became an internal fire, and I longed to scratch at it madly. To dunk my foot in a pail of ice water. I bit my tongue to keep from crying out but couldn't bear the burn silently.

I heard the other women cry out with me in unison at the flare of pain. Blessedly, I was able to close my eyes, tilted my head to the domed ceiling, and looked away from the perfection of the male specimens that cruelly appraised us.

It didn't last long. I was like a child who'd just been ordered not to stare at a horrific automobile accident. I *had* to look.

My chin dropped, and my eyes went to one man in particular. His platinum hair was loose and stuck straight over the broad shoulders of his charcoal grey suit. His pale brows furrowed, and the wide, icy gaze was smoldering into mine.

My air left in a whoosh, and a shiver shot down my spine. I had the sudden certainty that if I couldn't break his gaze, I would turn into a dry husk of papery skin and powdery bones, a mummified remnant of a young woman that had been ripped from her home and taken to God-only-knows where against her will. A pile of ashes in pooled, red silk. If I couldn't look away, I knew that I would happily begin to claw my own eyes out, a crazed part of me feeling blessed for being able to do so.

"Gentleman," a voice oozed behind me. A voice that I'd heard only briefly but was burned into my psyche forever. "As always, your presence is a great honor, and as promised, the product we have acquired for your pleasure is top-notch. I daresay that this will be our finest yet, and without having to leave the States. A couple I have even plucked myself."

Silence in answer, not a rustle of silk from the stage or the creak of a theater-style chair from the audience. The creature's — for there was no way he was a mere man — eyes burned into mine for a moment longer, and I felt what had to be the beginnings of insanity.

My overwhelmed brain sputtered, then I was whisked away from the moment, recalling my childhood — the day I'd found my dog, Lucy, with her innards gleaming red and her teeth scattered across the pavement after she was hit by a semi doing roughly ninety miles per hour. The way her tail had twitched when, at only ten years old and with no one to mind me while my parents killed a case of *Bud-Light*, I'd knelt by her side, the asphalt digging into my threadbare leggings. I hadn't seen the car stop in the lane to my left, or the large, graying man that I'd later think resembled Santa swoop to my side and gather me up, gently depositing me on the unkempt grass of my lawn while I'd screamed, biting and scratching, insisting that Lucy needed me.

Santa had brushed the tangled, dirty hair from my face, his large nose red and oily and his white whiskers quivering with a look I now recognize as pity, and had gently guided me to my house. My father, drunk and in pajama bottoms, hadn't taken kindly to the man's tongue-lashing over his neglect.

Father had grabbed a gun.

Santa produced one from the back of his black coveralls.

My father had been shot in the foot that day, and the man who'd told me his name was Jim had buried Lucy while my mother had tearfully escorted my father to our pickup, glaring at me in such a way that I knew she'd wished I was in Lucy's place instead. Our closest neighbor had kept me for the night. She was a widow that smelled of cigarettes but was kindly and slipped me sweets a couple of times a week. Her name was Priscilla, and she collected porcelain dolls that seemed to watch me as I'd crept through the house littered with cat shit and dust bunnies the size of my fist.

I was crying, I knew, as scene after scene replayed in my mind. My broken foot in junior high, nightmares I'd wake from screaming as a teen that were played in HD quality, and heartbreakingly, perfectly clear recaps of Mitch and I, moving together, our foreheads pressed, our lashes entwined. The way his fingers clenched on my hip with his release, his breath momentarily taken away with my own. The crescents I'd left in his back and kissed later, welling with just the tiniest amount of blood.

I became stuck in one such memory.

Mitch glared at me, hazel eyes sparking. "I told you to let me drive. You suck at driving in snow. I know this. You know this, but no, you just had to insist, didn't you?"

He smacked the dashboard, smoke practically curling around his ears. In the dark interior of the rusty Chevy Impala, I couldn't see him, but I knew his face was beet red. His skin was wildly reactive to emotion, and he never got pissed without resembling a tomato. A very sexy, very edible tomato.

I rolled my eyes. "Maybe I could've focused on the road if you'd stopped yacking for two seconds about how suicidal it is to allow me behind the wheel if it isn't seventy-five degrees and sunny!"

I'd wanted ice cream. That's all. I'd wanted to drive myself to get ice cream, and Mitch had denied me, insisting he drove alone instead. The roads were dangerous, he'd said. I should stay home, safe and warm.

I'd felt like a child being told I was too young to stay up late and watch a television program. I'd raged.

After threatening to walk — and meaning it — my anger making me reckless, he'd relented, tossing me the keys and calling shotgun.

On the way home, I'd taken a curve too quickly, and we'd ended up in a ditch. Stuck. Waiting on a tow-truck that would charge two hundred bucks to haul us the short ten miles home.

I scrubbed my face with my hands, and Mitch hopped out for what felt like the twentieth time, shouting for me to gun the motor in reverse as he'd pushed and strained at the bumper. Hopping back inside in defeat and slamming the Impala's door so hard I wondered if it'd break off into large chunks of rusty metal, my cell had chirped. It was the tow guy. He'd be running late, he'd said. Stay tight, he'd assured. He'd only be an hour.

Mitch had bitten his knuckles, a wordless, strangled sound of frustration, making me jump.

"What a man-baby." I'd sneered. We rarely argued, but when we did, I was despicable. Knowing just what buttons to push to send Mitch into a seething rage that usually resulted in him leaving for a few hours. He was the one who used common sense when angered. He distanced himself. He allowed himself time to cool down.

There was no escape in the cab, and as pissed as he was, I knew he wouldn't leave me — abandon me here.

"And you" — he turned his head slowly — "are being a bitch."

I'd drawn back my hand, palm out, but before the blow could connect with his cheek, his hand had shot out, grabbing my wrist.

"No." One word, filled with anger and sadness and making me tremble.

"I-I . . ." I stuttered, a flood of shame making me drop my eyes.

"There are other ways to handle violent urges. We don't hit, Wren. No matter what happens, we never, ever raise a hand to one

another."

He'd grabbed my head then, his lips crushing hard against mine. I'd bitten his lip, drawing blood, fumbling with his puffy down coat. Mitch grabbed my thighs, squeezing, then slipped his hands down, tossing me onto my back, hand cupped behind my head. Wrestling with my snow boots, he tossed them onto the floor. After fumbling with the button of my jeans, he'd tore it off, the small disk making a tinging noise somewhere against the dash. The torn bench seat was rough against my back, but I didn't care. Tossing my panties onto the floor, he'd wrenched me roughly into his lap.

"Take off the fucking coat."

I obliged, hands trembling.

In one swift motion, he'd wrenched me up and onto his hardness, my back stiffening as he sank into me. My nails dug into the soft flesh at the back of his neck as I'd cried out at the delicious fullness. I'd sat for a moment, relishing the warmth of him inside of me, my hands finding his hair and pulling roughly. Mitch smiled up at me, his teeth flashing white in the darkness, feral, challenging, mine.

I wrenched his head back, my legs pumped until they burned, his hands cupped my ass, then moved to my hips, pounding me down hard on his length and sending shockwaves down my spine. Our tongues clashed wildly, and he moaned into my mouth with his release. I followed a second later, collapsing against him, a single tear running down my cheek.

"I'm sorry," I'd whispered as he'd stroked my hair.

I felt his smile against my cheek.

"Best apology I've ever had."

Later, when the tow man had arrived, I'd been disappointed.

From that day on, Mitch never protested when I drove in the snow, as long as he could come along.

I might have been there for years, as time had ceased to exist. Wrenched from the painfully clear flashback of Mitch, I felt my heart break anew.

Is this what happened when you died? Surely, my heart

couldn't stand any more of the dark fantasy that was now my life. Was I already dead? Was this heaven or hell?

Suddenly, being shackled in this building and being the cumrag of the staff wasn't sounding so bad — not if I had to look into the eyes of the man-thing that I knew had already claimed me for the remainder of my life.

I wondered if he could see into my head. I wondered if he paused on images and appraised intimate memories that I held sacred. I wondered if he scoffed at my lack of grace, at the scars only Mitch had kissed, at the million little things that we did when we believed we were alone. When we believed nobody was watching.

I'd never felt so tiny and insignificant in my entire life. The power that fizzled in this room left me gob-smacked and plummeting to the bottom of the food chain. The injection was making me oblivious, but it couldn't banish the despair as I tried to hang on to who I was and what was happening. The stark contrast of chemical joy and the flood of my grim reality was drowning me, pulling me into an abstract purgatory that should not exist.

We were not so clever after all.

I wondered how long they'd been visiting our world — or was it their world — and why they'd not taken over yet and made slaves of the entire human race.

I tried to scream, patting my throat with disbelief when no sound accompanied my cries. I glanced to each side of me, noting that the other girls were clutching their throats. The air filled with something musky, wild, and indescribable, making my nose itch.

Magic, the part of my brain still operational mused. *That smell is magic.*

The band on my ankle was warm, pulsing.

The hallucinations of the injection returned, and a glitter tornado manifested between the bidders and I. Little pink sparkles rained around me, landing on the heads of dozens of slithering, yellow-eyed snakes.

Not real, I reminded myself as they hissed and curled around my arms, my ankles. Nonetheless, I brushed them away, shrieking silently as they struck, fangs dripping with venom. The band on my ankle blazed.

Falling forward to my hands, I retched, but nothing came up. From the sounds of it, I wasn't the only one in the throes of a bad trip, and though the assuage of serpents had felt as if it'd lasted an eternity, from the looks of our seated, terrifyingly beautiful guests, not much time had passed at all. They appeared just as calm and mildly bored as before, and I had to look away quickly, as staring at them physically hurt my eyes as if I were staring into the sun.

One woman smacked her head over and over, clawing and pulling at her earlobes until they bled. Though silent, the word her mouth formed over and over was unmistakable.

Bugs

It was over as quickly as it began.

No numbers were called.

No one spouted off the lightning-fast gibberish of an auctioneer.

My handsome kidnapper stood beside each of us, moving along in single file. When behind a new woman, he'd nod, acknowledging the creatures in the crowd, his eyes darting to and fro. Some kind of silent communication taking place.

They're bidding telepathically here in Narnia's sewers.

I watched with morbid fascination, doing my best to avoid the eyes of the silent marvels in the crowd, thankful that my imaginary snakes had been replaced by dozens of snow-white Persian kittens that chased one another across the stage, bouncing playfully, batting and pouncing one another.

My captor now stood behind me, spending more time at my back than any of the other women so far. I watched the crowd, my eyes darting wildly, watching for any hint of who might be claiming me now.

One of them smiled, and my blood ran cold.

I knew who'd won.

The one who'd been watching me since we'd been led to the stage.

The women were quickly pulled away by the lackeys and placed in front of their new owners, some screaming, some weeping, some silent and grinning, clearly gold-tripping.

A woman with a long, white ponytail in what appeared to be a summer dress that shimmered like a rainbow mirage materialized from the shadowy recesses behind the men-that-were-not-men, carrying a black tray with what resembled chutes of champagne, but with tiny black lids on the top. More women, just as beautiful, followed with matching trays, each with varying amounts of tubes. As the woman in the sundress all but floated slowly closer to the stage, I could see that the contents of the containers were a vibrant, glowing sky-blue and were animated, as if tiny, invisible fish were swimming inside. I blinked, and then it was the soft orange of a sunset with accents of yellow and pink.

I was next.

I should have been weeping or pleading, but I was strangely resigned. I didn't know if it was the gold liquid or just cold acceptance, but I didn't fight when a hot hand clamped around the cool skin of my arm and unceremoniously guided me toward the end of the stage.

My new owner lifted one large, golden hand and crooked a finger, a small smile playing on his full lips.

Aliens, I thought as I shifted my gaze from his finger to his face, my eyes brimming when they made contact with his for a split-second.

I barely felt the hands gripping my shoulder as I teetered on the icepicks that somehow passed for footwear. My spine rigid, I forced my eyes wide, arm in arm with a large black man in scrubs who had a teardrop tattoo on his upper cheek.

I descended the trio of shiny steps, careful to avoid looking at the other women and their new owners, fearing their hysterical reactions might feed my own.

But when the hired hand and I came to a stop, I looked boldly into the face of the thing that wanted to take me to whatever hell it'd come from.

My breath whooshed out as a tidal wave of power forced me to my knees, and my ankle-band seared my flesh.

Beautiful. Oh, God. I could use every pretty word in the dictionary to describe him, and each would fall pitifully short. No artist could have created such exquisite cheekbones or the fine cleft in the strong chin. His skin was so delicate and perfectly sun-kissed it was almost feminine. It glowed faintly, reminding me of paintings of holy saints, as if his aura was so pure that it couldn't be contained within. Fair, thick brows arched gracefully over eyes that seemed to swirl with pinpricks of white light as his gaze raked over me. One corner of his mouth twitched up, just for a moment, bringing my attention to his lower lip, dimpled in the middle and the pale pink of peony. The upper was full as well, with a tiny sliver of a scar denting it near the right corner. His hair was pulled back from his wide, strong brow and fell thickly over one broad shoulder in a braid nearly the width of my wrist, and he flicked it away from his suit dismissively. He splayed his large body, then his legs parted, one hand coming up to absently stroke his jaw. A solitary silver hoop adorned his left ear, and he pulled at it once, his mouth spreading into a lazy smile while I wondered if my eyes were going to explode from my skull.

I couldn't look away.

I would go blind if I couldn't.

"Crawl and show me how submissive you can be," he ordered softly.

I fell forward onto my hands, crawling forward, tears

falling soundlessly onto the carpet. My trembling hands reached his knees, then his thighs. I raised my head, my neck blazing as I struggled to keep it down.

I couldn't. And damn his eyes, they were sparkling with what looked like amusement. He released a rumbling laugh, and I felt his hand in my hair, gently massaging my scalp.

"It will not be painful for you. You'll be well cared for."

His voice was velvet. The accent was unfamiliar, like French, but not quite. Music. I don't know what I'd expected. Telepathy? A series of beeps and clicks? Some high speech from another world that my human brain couldn't translate, maybe.

"Stand. We're leaving." It was an order, said with what sounded like complete confidence.

The fire left my ankle band, and with it, the force that manipulated my body.

I flew backward onto my ass, palms splayed, pushing away from him, lungs burning and on the verge of hyperventilation. I looked behind me to see a lone woman, screaming obscenities and trying in vain to wrestle away from the lackeys, being dragged back through one of the doors we'd entered. I guess she hadn't made the cut.

I stood, all right.

I stood and bolted.

Right into the chest of the thing that had been seated a split second before.

Impossible. Yet there he was, and my God, was he ever tall.

It was like barreling into a slab of stone, and I flew backward, my heels toppling beneath me, my arms pinwheeling. I didn't see him move, but he was suddenly there, his hand on the small of my back, his brows furrowing, and the force of his stare piercing me. The air exploded from my chest, and I gritted my teeth, trying to break eye contact. I felt wetness on my cheeks, and I reached up, the pads of my fingers coming away a sticky scarlet.

He pulled me upright, and I looked down, my shoulders tensed with an effort to keep from whipping my head up and drinking in the beauty of him as I cried blood like a Virgin Mary statue.

"You will not try that again." The command rocked me as if he'd physically shaken me, and I reached out, grasping the breast of his suit so that it wouldn't send me reeling backward again. His voice was thunder in my head, and my vision blackened at the edges. I sagged, barely holding myself up, and he made no move to support me. He was breathing heavily, and the air I breathed tasted metallic. Wrong.

Perhaps he'd break my neck after all.

I made a mental note to bolt at every goddamn opportunity.

His hand was on the back of my head, his fingers dug into my hair. He jerked my head back, and I shut my eyes with every ounce of my will, the lids twitching, though my irises were evidently happily willing to be fried.

"Will you?" he asked, deceptively soft, though lightning bolts might as well have been dancing around my feet, cracking the floor beneath me in jagged lines.

I forced the words between my gritting teeth, hissing as his fingers pulled my tresses firmer. "Is the sky blue, asshole?"

I was thrown over his shoulder, my dress hitching up dangerously high, my legs kicking. I don't know why he didn't use his mind-mojo to make me docile because I was clawing at his back like a cat on cocaine.

I craned my neck, struggling to spot my dark-haired kidnapper in the throng of lackeys and the otherworldly men now mingling on the stage. A recent memory surfaced — the nurse with the severe bun and prickly attitude who'd had bathroom duty. Her arms casually resting on the bed frame.

Faye special.

The Faye. As in, the race of myth that had been stealing

children and making humans dance until they died, kinda Faye? I eyed the strange men behind us for a second, the white hair, the iridescent eyes, the glow. My original captor was now chatting animatedly with the woman carrying the tray of color-changing liquid and examining one of the vials. He grinned like a possum with a lollipop.

Payment for the products, I presumed.

I focused again on making myself as much of a nuisance as possible, arms flailing wildly, screeching every curse word I could recall and creating new ones. His graceful steps didn't falter, and annoyed, I curled my fingers into talons, digging them into his shoulders with all my might.

He paused, going still. He lifted his arm for a moment, and I sucked in air greedily. The ache in my stomach was alleviated for a moment without the pressure of his hold. I teetered without his grip, thought about leaping at the expense of my face smacking the floor, but swiveled my neck instead, alarmed. His hand was raised, palm slightly curled.

The smack on my ass sounded like thunder in the auditorium and jarred my teeth. I shrieked, arching my back, sure my stomach would be majorly sore the next day, if I lived that long.

"You'll reserve the scratching for different circumstances. For right now, you'll behave." He reprimanded me in a tone that suggested he was speaking to a naughty pet.

"Like hell!" I roared.

There was pressure against my crown, and then the spindly tendrils were digging in, probing, wormy. I whimpered as the warmth returned, waiting for my will to be obliterated.

"This, then?" he questioned, soft, sultry.

I stilled. My voice was small. "No."

I went limp as the warmth receded, knowing that I'd been a few seconds away from losing control over every part of my body. Maybe he would've made me use his body like a stripper pole.

"A pity." But I could hear the smile in his voice, and I shuddered as his hand smoothed over my spine.

I didn't bother to look at my surroundings, staring blankly at the floor, my arms hanging loosely. One of my heels had dropped at one point, and my new owner had barked at an unseen individual to retrieve it. When the other fell off, he merely sighed. A minute later, we came to a stop. With deceptive gentleness, my new owner lifted my body as if it were weightless. He tucked me close as I slid down his body, my hands on his broad chest. I noted the steady, strong beat of his heart beneath my palm and checked off the suspicion that he was one of the undead.

I wouldn't stare into that face again. I would not be arrested by the eyes that could hypnotize more effectively than the snake in *Jungle Book*.

"Look at me." The command was soft but instantaneous in its effect on my range of motion.

My eyes worked slowly up his chest, noting for the first time how very tall he was — my head barely crested his breastbone. His lips were parted slightly, and squinting, I met his gaze. I expected my eyes to burn, to bleed, but the pain never came. The pale ice iris seemed to swirl with purple tendrils, as if his small, violet pupils were the eye of a hurricane.

"Yes, I can turn it down and completely off. How often that can happen is entirely up to your behavior. This is better, no?"

I said nothing but could have sagged with relief that his voice no longer raked over me like warm hands, killing all thought. The voice was still beautiful, yes, but it no longer forced my mind to bend at angles that threatened to leave me drooling and vacant.

Others were around us. All the chosen women. I realized I was the only one without a dopey smile. One woman, a gorgeous Latino with a glittering, rubied tiara and a pale blue gown with voluminous skirts, was caressing her bosom with a look of pure ecstasy, her eyes trained on her owner — a God-like slab of man with short, spiky platinum hair and a row of golden hoops all along the edge of his ear. He cupped her chin, grinning rakishly, watching her self-fondling with obvious delight.

He glanced up before I could look away, and our eyes locked. My knees weakened instantly, and I felt my feet begin to shuffle in his direction, the band around my ankle heating.

"Audious!" The thing that'd bought me barked, but he sounded far away, his hand grasping the back of my neck as if I were a straying kitten.

The spiky-haired one laughed, looking away, and the hold was immediately broken. I stumbled back, my hand flying to my chest.

"I think I prefer yours, Tarove." Audious smiled. "She likes me. I can tell."

"Another word and your purchase will be mine, as well," Tarove growled.

That shut Audious up. The Latino never noticed. She was in the process of removing the straps of her gown.

"What the fuck is this?" I barked. "What in the actual fuck is all of this? What are you people? Are you even people? Where are you taking us?" I was in danger of being zapped by Tarove's invisible sexy-time laser, but I didn't care.

"We're your God's now." Audious purred, staring at my feet and working his gaze up. "We're your Alpha's and you're Omega's. And mortals don't address God's with such audacity."

"And you are a dickhead," a male voice somewhere off the right quipped.

To hear strange beings that, for all I know had teleported here from another planet, make jabs at one another with such human insults somehow made the situation all the more overwhelming. I swayed, one hand going to my temple, my face crumpling as tears burned the back of my eyes.

"I'm going to be sick." I groaned to no one and everyone.

A strong arm snaked around from behind me, pulling me back gently. My back pressed against a solid chest, and I could feel his muscles rippling as he bent down, his lips brushing my ear, causing an involuntary shiver to raise goosebumps on my skin that had nothing to do with my nausea.

"Only a moment longer, and we will be alone," he said like a vow, as if that would fill me with comfort. I wished I could puke at will. I watched the Latino woman dancing now, her moves sinuous. Audious clapped to a beat I couldn't hear. A grunt behind me, and a large hand cupped my chin, turning my head away.

"Don't," he said softly, with some unreadable emotion in his voice.

"Portal the hell up," Audious growled, pushing the Latino roughly away. I tore my chin out of the hand to look towards him, my cheeks reddening. The Latino was naked from the waist up. A wave of pity made my fingers curl, the ragged ends biting into my palms, and I wondered if she was scream-ing inside as she stumbled after him, making soft, needy sounds in her throat.

Audious spread his arms wide, his head tilted back, and I watched as narrow beams of silver light shot from the tips of his fingers. Laughing, he curled the digits inwards, bringing them down with his arms in front of him in a *Superman* pose. Uncurling his fingers, the light left him, snaking through the air almost playfully until the individual slivers of lumines-cence converged, taking on the shape of an orb. The orb grew quickly, and I shielded my eyes, unable to look away, and my jaw unhinged in wonder.

An explosion of light had me crying out, covering my face. I wondered if this was the final straw — if my peepers would succumb to this latest abuse and refuse to work after I opened them again. But as the light beyond my eyes retreated, I peeked again, my curiosity stronger than my fear.

The orb was now a square-shaped door of light in front of Audious and appeared to be suspended upright by nothing. White vapor rolled out from the bottom of it, and the room dropped at least thirty-degrees.

"That's cool as shit!" a slurred female voice exclaimed, followed by a high-pitched giggle. "Let's go to *Neverland* bitches!"

"Will you shut her up?" A man to my left said. He had his gleaming hair gathered in a very tidy bun and the underside shaved. "I nearly chose that one. Gods be thanked that I did not. Miana will disembowel her in a week."

"That's far too messy," A softer, masculine voice said. "Miana will not risk staining her slippers. She'll force me to do it."

There was laughter all around as my mind was blown to smithereens. Then the door glowed even brighter. I was breathing way too fast, my palms sweaty, but still so very aware of the firm body behind me and the hand drawing circles around my navel through the material of my gown. I considered wrenching it into my mouth and giving him the *Scars* treatment, but my weariness and shock left me staring straight ahead, feeling as if I'd slip from my body and float away. There was too much information turning my brain to mush. Only anger remained. Bright and pulsing. Bidding me to wait until the time was right to unleash it.

At that moment, it hit home that I would never see Mitch again. Not in this life.

I leaned back against my new master, shivering, uncaring that he probably took my closeness as a sign that I'd accepted my new status as a pet. I didn't care what he thought. He might as well have been a wall. I tilted my head back, my eyes on the plain white ceiling, my jaw clenched. I mentally called Mitch's name, willing it beyond the confines of this place, through the ceiling, and out into the universe. I didn't know how many miles separated us, but I prayed to God that he would broadcast my love to the man of my dreams one final time before I went to whatever lay beyond the door.

A hand upon my jaw forced my gaze back to the door.

"Mourn your mortal life later. For now, watch."

As the light forced me to squint, I focused on my disgust and the hate that I was shoveling fueled darkness into with reckless speed. I burned from within, grinding my teeth as one of the well-dressed beings and his new plaything stepped through the door of light.

I felt Tarove stiffen, his hand tightening on my lower jaw. Had this man-thing sensed the darkness I nursed like the dead child I would never hold? Did he realize that he'd purchased his own demise? God. I hoped so.

Like I'd promised myself before. My new master would die by my hand.

I watched the couples disappear one by one—eleven in total—into the square of pulsing, brilliant light. Tarove's large hands smoothed down to my shoulders, and his breath was hot on my ear as he urged me forward.

"There are other dimensions . . . thousands of them . . . though we'll only pass through three. I'm very confident that you'll survive the trip."

His words bounced around in my brain, meaning little. Alarm skittered across my flesh, but it was muted. My chest rising and falling, I tilted my head back, looking up at him.

"So there's a possibility that I may not make it back to your cave?"

He chuckled, and I faced the light again, playing with the notion of digging my heels in and screaming like a banshee. I wanted to beg and throw myself at his mercy, and his kiss shoes that could very well have been made from the hide of garden gnomes. But to do so would have shown weakness. Vulnerability.

I'd displayed enough of that in the past couple of nights.

There wasn't any getting out of this. The band around my ankle was obviously some type of conduit to Tarove and his ilk, and fighting the inevitable would only result in my trailing after him like a puppy, or — I shivered as I recalled the topless Latina — much, much worse. I'd find a way to remove the band if I survived the trip, I vowed, and by whatever means necessary. I wondered if his kind were still capable of manipulating humans without the band, and I pushed the bubble-bursting thought away. I clutched my pitiful shred of hope, locking it in the pretty pink box full of Mitch's kisses and dreams of a happy family.

The scene from *Saw* wasn't looking so farfetched now. I'd happily saw away my own foot if I could be free of the evil band that could put me on my ass in a heartbeat.

My breath now left in frosty, white plumes, and I'd begun to shiver as cold air seeped rudely through the thin silk of my dress. My teeth began to chatter, loudly in my head.

"There's nothing beyond the realm of possibility after we step through the portal, little kit." I could hear the smile in his voice, and a warm ripple slid down my spine, though the band around my ankle remained cool. What kind of being was he that his mere voice could act as a powerful stimulant? I recalled fairy tales of Sirens leading the captains of ships to their watery doom. I wondered if he was in the same family of freaks.

My shivering became close to convulsive as tiny, light-infused pieces of what appeared to be snow pelted my exposed skin. His warm hands smoothed down my arms, my spine going ramrod straight in response as his hot mouth gently nipped at my ear. Without warning, I was scooped into his arms, tucked close against his unnaturally warm chest.

"A precaution, in case you decide to fling yourself to your doom in a romantic gesture."

"Why not just use the band to ensure that doesn't happen?" I gasped, snot disgustingly freezing to my upper lip. I snuggled closer to his heat, though it goaded me to no end. "Why let my trying to escape be a possibility at all?"

His voice was indulging. "Because I believe we have an understanding, and I like this preventive measure much better." He squeezed me closer for a moment, and I made a sound of disgust.

"I'll never understand a monster." I sniffed. I was forced to turn my face towards his heat, burying it into his suit. The scent of honeysuckle and ice filled my nose as intense and unnatural cold savagely beat at my exposed skin. I would be close to hypothermia soon, I guessed. It didn't matter, though my body traitorously sought a source of heat.

He walked, cradling me, and the tears that leaked free froze on my lashes in fat icy drops, obstructing my vision. I cried out, the burn of the elements not unlike fire.

A loud buzzing that reminded me of the hornet's nest that'd hung beneath an old sycamore in our yard as a child vibrated my eardrums. My father had thought it clever to shoot the large, grey cone with his twenty-two, and after he'd been stung roughly twelve times, we'd all cowered in the house, hornets covering the screen door. Their large, black and yellow striped bodies were twitching, large stingers gyrating and eager to puncture flesh. They'd multiplied until they'd blocked the light from beyond the outside entirely. Then they found their way through a small hole in the screen and began to cover the glass of our main door, buzzing with rage near the cracks. My mother had called the authorities, and she and I had been forced to stay at a hotel while my father was nursed in the hospital. His face was swollen grotesquely, smiling as if he'd accomplished something commendable. As if he hadn't nearly killed us all. He hadn't been smiling when his eyes had finally swollen shut, and much to my mother's dismay, his throat. He'd nearly succumbed to shock.

He'd deserved it, I thought, as I watched as a fine layer of ice formed on my curled hand. My father had ruined the creatures' home. He'd killed their larvae.

He deserved that and more.

CHAPTER SEVEN: THE OTHER

The buzz amplified, and now it was in my flesh, my bones. My teeth vibrated against one another, my eyes feeling as if they'd leave their nerves and tumble from their sockets. I cried out, my back arching against Tarove's arms, ice cracking and sliding from my fingers as I fisted them in my hair and began to pull. I waited for my joints to be dislocated, for my blood to congeal, turning to thick sludge in my veins.

Tarove was shouting something, his ever-warm fingers biting into my skin as a tempest blasted us, cold and unforgiving. My lips immediately chafed raw, and I inhaled tiny crystals that formed inside of my nose. Closing my eyes against the burn, lest they freeze in their sockets, I held my breath. My hair tangled around my face, so stiff with ice that it felt like tiny switches as it battered my cheeks.

I don't know when I lost consciousness, but when I woke, it was to blessed silence.

A hot, balmy breeze that smelled faintly of mint and something like pine began to melt the ice in my hair, which hung wildly around me, clumped with what was now slush. My lips burning, I gaped like a fish, releasing my hold on Tarove's suit and staring around me in wonder. I searched for the other couples, and not seeing a trace of them, assuming they'd gone ahead of us.

Large, palm-like trees, heavy with emerald fruit shaped like the human heart, swayed on each side of us, and as I watched, a creature no bigger than my hand popped its head out of the tree directly to our left. Lime-green feathers — their shape reminiscent of dandelion petals — framed a monkey-like, cinnamon face with perfectly round, half-dollar-sized eyes. The tail, standing at attention, was thin and covered in fine, matching green downy. The branch the creature hovered in trembled as the thing hurled a piece of fruit from its tiny fist, which bounced off the side of Tarove's head.

Tarove glared.

The creature began a high-pitched wailing, its siren-screech making me cover my ears. The beast shook the fronds of the tree angrily, pausing only to hoot in a deep baritone before resuming the screech again. Its mouth opened wide while small, triangle-shaped teeth gleamed wetly.

I wondered what kind of damage those teeth could do on soft, human flesh as other heads began to emerge from the palms, reminding me of the *Whack-a-Mole* game. Fruit dropped and burst on the ground like overripe melons as they shook the trees angrily, the fronds waving and whispering, welcoming us to this strange new world full of adorable little bird-monkeys that appeared to be in agreeance that we were not welcome.

I glanced at the lavender sky, gaping at the two large, ping-pong ball smooth twin moons hanging amid juniper clouds, and felt my mind beginning to unravel.

Oh, Nelly. Goodbye, mind. Hello, batshit.

Tarove walked calmly, seemingly unconcerned with the three creatures that were now running circles around us, pelting us with broken pieces of the red, mushy fruit. A delicious, citrusy scent surrounded us, and I turned my head as a piece slapped against my cheek, dripping. I swatted it away as I spat out the indescribable sweetness that had seeped into my mouth, vaguely wondering if it was poisonous.

"Oh my God!" I couldn't help myself. I began to flail in Tarove's arms, close to climbing on his shoulders, anything to get away from the tiny devil's that were like nothing I'd seen on earth. They were swarming us now, gnashing their teeth, their deep, hooting raising the hairs on the back of my neck. Their war dancing commenced, and their cries grew louder as they danced closer on all fours, their paws dainty and kitten-like.

"They're nesting nearby. They see us as a threat to their offspring. Nasty, feces-flinging varmints."

One of them launched itself into the air as if bouncing from a tiny trampoline and hung from the toes of my right foot, flashing those wicked teeth, eyes gleaming. Tarove's hand shot out in a blur, grasping the angry beast by its slender throat, and with one shake of his big, golden hand, a soft crack announced its demise. Tarove tossed its limp, little form into the mob of its brethren, one of its face-framing feathers floating softly on the sticky breeze.

"Now you've done it! They're going to eat us alive, you cretin!" I shrieked, my sodden hair clinging to my face.

Tarove laughed, leaning close, as if a hundred exotic, pissed-off space-monkeys were of little concern. "What are the meat-eating fish from your world called? The species that can reduce a grown man to gristle and bone in moments if he wanders into their watery territory? Pir-yantas?" Pirkantas?"

He was fucking with me.

I shrieked as another creature launched itself towards us, ripping the hem of my flimsy dress and growling as it shook its head like a Pitbull. There were ragged ribbons of silk hanging from its teeth. Tarove backhanded it away almost casually, and the rest of my fake nails snapped on his suit in my scramble to seek higher ground. The space-monkeys were hopping in place now in unison, hooting in sync as they crowded closer.

"The *Autukay* are much like your *Porantas*, but the world is their river."

"Piranha's!" I gasped. "Piranha's, you oof!"

"There's a strong possibility more will congregate, what with your smelling so very scrumptious. I'd imagine it's an aphrodisiac to their bloodlust. The stink of your fear likely carries for miles."

I punched his shoulder, hard, tears welling in my eyes as the little demons below switched from hoots to that godawful screeching.

"It's not enough that you bought me, that you bastards killed my baby, and that you use mind-control to make me obedient, but you also get off on scaring the hell out of me. I hate you! I hate all of you!"

Unmistakable confusion flashed across his face, lips parting. He studied me, chaos exploding around us as fruit launched in all directions.

"I was not informed that you'd been with child. Such information is agreed to be given upfront, before the auction takes place. Reason being" — he paused, catching an *autukay* mid-air just before it landed on his left shoulder, and snapping its neck, tossing it behind him with a disgusted grimace — "is that forced removal of life often leaves the product with lingering feelings of grief and anger, which often bleeds onto the new owners, creating dysfunction." He walked unhurriedly now, seemingly oblivious to the monkey-beast gnawing his shoulder through his suit.

Product. As if I were the latest mobile phone model.

I drew back my left hand and curled the fingers into a tight fist, ready to ruin his perfect nose, but I never got the chance. Warmth slithered from the top of my crown, and the band on my ankle heated uncomfortably. I bit my tongue, my fist shaking, frustrated tears leaking from the corners of my eyes.

He stopped walking.

"We're here." He smiled. "This realm houses a shortcut through the halls. Luckily, the portals are rarely far from one another. They're symbiotic. One cannot sustain itself far from the other. In worlds with double-portals, if one disappears — and that's usually by Faye magic — the other will seal itself as well, locking us out from that dimension. We could have simply stayed in the hall and walked a bit longer, but I felt you could use a bit of distraction, and the weather is lovely here." Tarove's eyes twinkled down into mine, his jaw set, lips pursed. I tore my eyes away from his.

The ankle band cooled, and I let my arm drop, defeated, letting my head loll back and allowing the tears to flow freely.

"I hate you," I whispered, biting my lip until the coppery taste of blood reached my taste buds.

"It's of no matter, and I'm well aware," he answered stiffly.

Lifting my head, I saw that the white glow of the new portal lit his face, making his platinum hair glow. "Does the horse despise its rider in your world? Does the cow loathe the farmer?"

I laughed bitterly and closed my eyes as the ice glazed over me.

Shivering and queasy, I hoped that my brain wouldn't shut my body down as the satanically-low buzz of the portal assaulted my ears, working its barbed way into my brain. Back arching, I willed myself to remain silent as I waited for the misery to reach a crescendo, but instead, it began to ebb. I cracked one eye, shivering in the cold as my already-dampened dress began to stiffen with ice. Tarove was on the move, his eyes intense.

"Keep your eyes on me if you don't wish to have nightmares for the rest of your tragically short life." He grunted.

"I've already got that covered, thanks to you," I said with as much venom as I could muster with chattering teeth.

"The travel will be less painful for you each time. Your cells weren't screaming in violent agony this time, no? Proof that even simple creatures can adapt when it's necessary."

I ignored him and took a deep breath.

We walked down a tunnel of sorts, its membranous, grey walls glistening with fat, red ropes that looked for all the world to be veins.

The bizarre tunnel *breathed,* and I wondered if we were in the belly of a monster—like Jonah inside of the whale. The perversely slick walls shuddered as a low moan drowned out the sound of Tarove's feet stepping wetly, the fleshy ceiling above us bowing.

I gasped. Portals. Hundreds of them. Stretching for as far as the eye could see.

Someone or something screamed.

I found myself nestling against Tarove again. My horror was so great that I took comfort in his strange otherworldliness, which paled in comparison to whatever I'd been seeing. His hair brushed my cheek, and I turned to stare into those icy eyes, his violet pupils expanding as his gaze met mine. I touched my cheek, then peeked at my fingertips, which were blessedly blood-free. One of his pale brows arched, amused.

"The distance from the portal from your world to the one we just visited was shorter, but you were unconscious for most of the journey. Would you like me to help you rest? I can feel your heart racing through your back. Are you prone to the vapors?"

"It's alive." I breathed, looking around at the tunnel, mystified.

He sighed. "In a sense."

"It's breathing. Places shouldn't breathe."

"As most living things do, though the *Other* isn't sustained by oxygen."

"Is it . . . aware?" I squeaked.

"Yes, and fickle." He smiled humorlessly, his gaze darting, looking wary for the first time.

I didn't probe further, the implications making me

nauseous as I tried to press myself closer to his hard chest. He sniffed. He was done enlightening me.

We passed close to a portal on the left, and it was slightly rounder than the others and pulsing with a dark swamp-green. An arm shot out, as yellow as a school bus and as thick as my waist. Three, horny fingers, stem-like and hyper-flexible, strained towards us, causing the fat pimples covering the flesh to burst and ooze a clear, jelly-like substance. Tarove danced away lightly, sighing. My shrieking and the stream of curse words that followed afterward echoed hollowly down the tunnel. I looked behind us just as the portal sucked the arm back in, shooting out a spray of a black, tar-like goo that sizzled as it made contact with the glistening, meaty floor.

"You'd been warned to keep your eyes closed."

I didn't answer, and he gave no warning before he stepped through a jagged portal on the right that glowed a soothing lavender.

The following bite of ice was anything but soothing, and after we'd stepped through, I launched into a coughing fit, not bothering to turn my head. Tarove looked down on me with what appeared to be an annoyance as my spittle sprinkled his face, and if my teeth hadn't resumed their chattering and pinching of my cold tongue, I might have smiled at my small victory. His eyes swirled, and I squinted my own shut. My band warmed slightly, and I felt his fingers curl into my rib-cage.

"We're making a pitstop."

CHAPTER EIGHT: DIRTY DANCING

I slowly took in my surroundings, unable to stop myself from gasping. The unmistakable tangy scent of salty seawater filled my lungs. I squinted at the twin, orange suns hanging over the crimson body of water that stretched endlessly towards a horizon marked with puffy, animated clouds that seemed to chase one another, bursting and rebuilding, then twining with their neighbors like serpents. Pulsing with light, the clouds broke again, causing little tendrils to stretch like the arms of reluctant lovers as they parted until they spun into another close by. The azure sky glittered with kaleidoscope stars of colors I couldn't name, scattering across its canvas.

The beach itself was a smooth, unblemished white, turning pink only briefly as waves lapped at its edge, seemingly stain-proof to the bloody caress of the sea. Behind us, colorful, thick vegetation arched into rocky formations choked with vines. Even at a distance, the colorful blooms on them were visible, hanging fat in countless hues of pink and purple.

The alien chitters and hoots of the jungle echoed frantically, and I pushed at Tarove's chest without looking at him, tumbling onto white, powdery sand sprinkled with clumps of nearly transparent grass.

I crawled, the sand sticking to my damp palms and knees, my ankle band cool.

I came to an abrupt stop as feet manifested in front of me, inches from my nose, only a shade or two darker than the sand. Slender feet. Feminine.

Working my gaze up slowly from fine-boned ankles and thin, almost colt-like calves, then onto the edges of a grassy, blue skirt that whipped like hair in the tropical, balmy breeze, I trembled. Wrenching my gaze upwards, I was unable to suppress a small scream. Two eyes, placed where the human belly button would be, stared at me from a flat stomach with sensuously rounded hips. Sea-glass green, the whites clear and the pupil an ordinary black, the lash-less eyes twitched to and fro, taking in my face. I forced my gaze up to small breasts — where they should be — decorated with tiny, brilliant gems the same hue as the grassy skirt the form wore. The gems spiraled decoratively at the center where the nipples should be but weren't.

Intricate jewelry in shining silvers and buttery gold flowed down the form's chest, hanging heavily from the abnormally long, slim neck. The female was bald, but with a crown of blood-red flowers not unlike carnations from our world, and I saw that the only set of eyes it possessed were on its tummy. Blank, and as smooth as its forehead, there were no indentations where the sockets should be. But the creature had a very human-like nose and a full, pouty mouth. White teeth flashed, causing the high cheekbones to look more pronounced, and I released my breath, thankful that they weren't razor sharp, and realizing I'd half-expected them to be,

"Oh, holy shit." I breathed.

The female-thing held a smooth, black stick — nearly as tall as she was — and decorated with tiny bones, bells, trinkets, and bits of brightly colored string.

More of the creatures materialized out of thin air. All of them with eyes in the wrong places, all of them scantily dressed, and all of their tummies turned towards me.

"Tarove," the female in front of me purred, then, taking a deep breath, she launched into a long string of some musical language that was unlike anything I'd heard on earth. She punctuated certain words with whistles and soft, sighing noises that rose and dropped in pitch. One of her hands, tattooed with crimson rune-like symbols, animatedly moved as she talked. The smile on her eyeless face was brilliant, and the eyes on her belly shined and squinted in obvious pleasure, causing the skin on her firm abdominals to crinkle.

My sanity was exploding into curly confetti. I could feel it. I waited for my brain to begin leaking from my ears.

The rest of the tribe stood eerily silent and still, but several smiled, leaning on their own gaudily decorated sticks.

Tarove responded in the native's strange language, and I could hear the familiarity in his voice as he moved closer behind me. Ever-so-gently, I felt him work his fingers into my hair, and with a slow tug, he eased me backward until I sat on the balls of my bare feet.

I didn't resist. I couldn't move by myself. I couldn't speak. I couldn't blink or tear my eyes away from the incomprehensible beings surrounding us.

My arms hung limply at my sides as I stared at the female's stomach, appalled and filled with the crazed need to poke one of the green orbs with my index finger.

Tarove's hand left my hair, gently massaging my shoulder. Looking slowly around, taking in both the male and females on this strange, new place, Tarove's voice began to sound far away, as if I was listening from underwater. My vision began to darken at the corners, and Mitch's face swam in from memory. He'd always loved the Sy-fy channel. I wished he could get a load of this crazy shit.

I was going to pass out.

Spontaneously I decided to make a run for it to see how far I could make it before the hoard of belly-gazing aliens descended upon me and beat me with their sticks. Maybe they'd truss me up and roast me over a spit.

Maybe Tarove would take a bite, too, after I was crisped to

perfection.

I leaned forward slowly, my eyes on the chatty female's belly pupils — which were focused on Tarove — and if I didn't know better, shining with adoration. As if sensing my stare, the orbs cut towards me sharply.

She held up one tattooed hand, and marvels upon marvels, she addressed me in beautifully accented English. "Your fear is unwarranted, Kelly, nor would you make it far."

Though, at this point it shouldn't have, the fact that she'd seemingly plucked my thoughts directly out of my mind shocked me. And given that it was coming from an anatomically incorrect being from a planet with two suns and a sea of blood, and I felt the few remaining hairs that weren't standing at attention on the back of my neck stiffen.

I felt dozens of misplaced eyes on my face, and I shivered.

The female's laugh tinkled like bells. "Come, Tarove. The tea is ever-the-ready and is sweeter than is usual."

I looked behind me, and his grin was all sorts of devilish.

"I haven't tasted it in many years, and I grow restless. Will there be music?"

The female nodded. "Your purchase is lovely," she remarked, stepping closer, one hip jutting as her midsection eyes raked over me. One hand reached out, and light as a butterfly, her fingers brushed my temple. I forced myself to meet her freaky eyes, though my own automatically wanted to search for them on her face instead. I breathed heavily, refusing to cringe as every muscle demanded.

"She is going to . . . a phrase from her world . . . be a *giant pain in the ass.* But . . . she is hurt. Deeply. Why would you buy such a broken being? It is a bit cruel. Do you grow malicious in your old age, Tarove? Next, do you beat the hounds? The maids?"

"As you can see, Maroosha, for I know you see far, I am not the one that damaged her. I wasn't aware of her . . . flaws.

Again, I am restless, and she is lively."

Maroosha threw back her head and laughed, the jewelry around her neck clinking. "Let us fetch the cups, then. I should see just how lively, indeed."

Something in my control snapped, and I shot to my feet, not liking the idea of subtropical magic tea being forced down my throat or the way the green belly-eyes had gleamed when speaking of it. I would run for the sea, I decided — fling myself into the waves, go limp, and breathe the crimson water without hesitation. A willing sacrifice to the sea monsters which no doubt dwelled there.

I made it one step before the damned band blazed. My body went stiff and my neck arched back, as if Tarove's hands were still buried in my hair. My arms turned to stone, heavy at my sides, and my knees threatened to cave under my weight. I swayed. His breath on my neck was hot, his voice rumbling. Heat spread from my scalp, dousing me in a fire that pulsed over zones that should have been the farthest thing from my mind.

"There's such a thing as *too* lively, and we're going to remedy that. For a while, at least." His tongue darted out as he sighed, flickering over my ear lobe. I shivered, my head dropping back further. My idiotic body responded to him as if I was still high with the Gold. I moaned, even as guilt screamed Mitch's name over the sound of my blood roaring in my ears.

I'd just left the love of my life in another dimension, lost my unborn child before I'd even been able to connect to the idea fully, and I was being dragged to a tea party with aliens against my will, and yet . . .

I couldn't deny the tingle that had nothing to do with the band. Heat made its languid way down my spine, and as the band around my ankle cooled, Tarove placed a slow, nibbling kiss on my neck, letting his lips rest for a moment just over my pulse.

I bit down on the tender flesh on the inside of my cheek, hard, tasting blood, and felt a black rush of anger. Twisting away, I spat red spittle onto the white sand below me. I couldn't help but stare as the fine grains promptly absorbed my DNA, returning to its original white perfection.

This was batshit.

"Don't touch me!" I said, backing up and glaring at him.

He stalked forward and, in one fell swoop, deposited me over his shoulder again. He used the band until we reached the small, dark brown huts further along the beach and, with the gentleness usually reserved for a sack of potatoes, deposited me on a woven, honey-colored mat on the ground.

I lost count of the huts, but if I'd had to make a guess, I'd have said maybe fifty of them dotted the area, some with smoke lazily wafting from holes in the top. Maroosha sat on a mat directly across from me, legs folded indian-style, head cocked, belly-eyes staring at me curiously. She tended a small fire, which sat a black, crude pot over the top. The contents boiled, and she stirred with a wooden spoon, mouth smiling.

After a few moments, an earthen bowl was placed in my hands, and a thin, fragrant liquid the color of beets was ladled into its belly. Tarove was given a bowl, as well.

"I'm *so* not drinking this. Why the hell would I ever? You actually expect me to voluntarily do this?" I asked Tarove incredulously, my heart in my throat. I sniffed the liquid experimentally. If I figured if it was toxic, I'd toss it back in one shot at this point.

"You could refuse, yes, but I can be very convincing."

The temperature of the atmosphere dropped immediately, and I shivered, the bowl remaining pleasantly warm in my hands as I gripped it tighter. Nightfall in this dreamscape apparently didn't creep—it pounced, draping its velvet hide around us hungrily. I searched for the twin suns hanging over the water and blared my eyes at the large, cratered, diamond-shaped moon in their place. It was suspended over the water, which now appeared black as onyx.

White, spindly things glowed in the waves as the tide crept closer, the creatures' movements slow and purposeful as they glided about others of varying sizes. The unblemished white of the sand all but disappeared as the sea crept unnervingly closer to our camp. I shivered, imagining terrifying versions of my Earth's locusts descending and for eyeless horsemen of the apocalypse to come bearing down, the hooves of their steeds dripping with salty crimson, the all-seeing orbs on their stomachs blood-red.

Torches flared to life simultaneously all around us, and a drum began to play — deep and tribal, beginning as the slow, laborious beating of a heart before more joined it, the beat becoming faster, hypnotic.

Maroosha smiled. "Drink." She raised her thumb to her lips, nipping the tip with her teeth. I watched as blood beaded on the surface, and I was horrified as she leaned over and coaxed a drop with the fingers of her other hand until it fell into my tea. She repeated the action over Tarove's drink.

"No way," I whispered as the drums reached a frantic pace, thrumming and heating my blood even as the chill of the night intensified. Maroosha's fire crept higher as if sensing my discomfort.

"I should hate to force you," Tarove said, watching me as he brought the bowl of disgustingness to his lips. The band in my ankle all but burst into a ring of fire.

The bowl pressed to my lips in a second flat, and I didn't so much as flinch as I finished the sweet, spicy liquid in two gulps. The taste was reminiscent of watermelon, and the faint coppery taste of Maroosha's blood was not at all repugnant, but as it settled in my belly, sweat popped out along my brow.

Dancing.

This tribe's inhabitants were dancing, and Tarove was

leading me gently to the bonfire, his hand warm. The purple flames swayed in time with the music, and as I watched, they transformed into the unmistakable shape of a man and a woman. Spinning and lifting their arms, they'd part only to collide, becoming one entity, curling and licking higher and higher, heads tossed back in fiery bliss.

"Dance with me," Tarove ordered, his cheek pressed against mine and his large hand heating my skin through the still-damp material of my dress.

"No," I said, refusing, even as I swayed to the beat.

This wasn't like the hallucinatory gold. No. Not at all. I wasn't high. I wasn't inebriated.

I was filled with passion, with *life*, and the overwhelming desire to move. Not away. No. Straight towards Tarove.

My arms snaked around his neck even as I shook my head in denial. "I'm getting sick of being drugged," I whispered.

"What makes the tea so very special isn't its intoxicating effects. It has none. It simply, and beautifully, magnifies your own desires as it coaxes them to the surface. You are doing exactly what you prefer in the back of your primitive brain right now, Kelly. And did I mention that, with the tea, one cannot tell a lie?"

I moaned miserably, wanting to extricate myself, but sure that if I did, I'd only stagger back, hungrier for his closeness than before.

"Do you want to dance with me, Kelly?" I was pressed so close to him now that my breasts ached. Pure, unfiltered danger seeped from him in thick, tempting waves, bidding me to test the waters.

I clamped my mouth shut.

The band warmed, and the phantom spiders tricked down my scalp and over my shoulders. I shot daggers at him with my eyes.

"Yes," I said, and with the admission came a small lick of

relief. An unburdening.

Icy eyes glowed briefly, his thick brows furrowing. My gaze went to the small scar on his upper lip, and I wondered what could mar a creature such as this. His platinum hair spilled loosely over his blazer, and while I watched, he shrugged it off, eyes swirling with small, violet hurricanes. The white cotton button-down shirt beneath followed, but without him lifting a finger. It simply vanished.

Woah.

"I dislike buttons." He grinned rakishly, obviously completely aware of how raw and sexual he looked in the fire's writhing glow.

He should've looked ridiculous when he began to sway in his black trousers. Then his shiny, dark leather shoes disappeared. His massive, muscled body should have looked awkward as his golden hands pushed his pale hair from his unlined brow and his shoulders rotated sensuously, but he looked anything but.

He looked as if he belonged in this bizarre wilderness by the bloody sea, with its glowing creatures playing tag in the waves and its oddly beautiful inhabitants. As if he could stalk into the jungle, scare away the biggest and worst of the monsters that likely lurked there, bare his teeth and beat his chest, all while maintaining the almost delicate beauty that marked his mysterious race.

His prominent, sculpted abdominals flexed as he moved. Arms almost entirely decorated with runes—not unlike those of Maroosha's—as he pulled me closer, his broad chest like a stone against my own. I wondered if he could feel my heart pounding against him. My eyes greedily raked over his shoulders and his chiseled jaw, and I felt myself weakening.

Faye.

They were pure sex, I decided. Sculpted by a bored Aphrodite when she needed something strange and tempting to curl about her celestial ankles. I pictured her running her glittering fingers through Tarove's hair and bidding him to bury himself in her star-struck guts and fuck her brains out.

The image made me strangely uncomfortable.

He wanted me to dance. A frumpy, damaged mortal that would kill him in his sleep if given half the chance when he could've had anyone, anywhere, in any strange dimension. I wondered if what he'd said was true. If the tea exposed the dirty desires lurking within one's psyche, compelling them to follow, and I allowed myself the small comfort of the possibility.

Looking at him, even as I hated him, even as I grieved the things I'd lost, how could anyone not desire him? I knew nothing about this man-thing. For all I knew, he was dragging me to a palace of horrors to be locked in a dungeon and whipped into oblivion when he was having a tedious day. Maybe straight into an abstract nightmare that would make hell look cheerful.

He'd made his clothing disappear in thin air, for god-sake.

I hadn't even seen a fraction of what he was capable of.

Maroosha spun by, trailed by a very tall male with violet eyes bulging from a firm, white belly. Laughing as the male nuzzled her neck, she pressed another bowl into my hands. Stepping away, my hips swaying in spite of myself, I threw it back in one gulp.

To hell with it.

From the looks of everything, I could very well be dead anyway and in the afterlife. If not, I'd reap whatever pleasure I could find. The tea was affecting me heavily, I knew. My hormones were in overdrive, but I was mentally exhausted and refused to fight it.

Denying Tarove was not an option, and as he swiveled his hips, hands behind his head, he looked better than any male stripper I'd ever seen. I pushed thoughts of my infidelity away, telling myself that, were Mitch in my position and

jacked up with the world's strongest *Viagra*, I would understand if he danced with a beautiful woman.

Especially if he concluded that his death was quickly ap-
proaching.

My skin flushed hotly, sweat collecting at my temples, and
I tossed my head back, arms moving sinuously above my
head. With the soft sand beneath my feet, I glided towards
Tarove, my lips parted. I glanced at the fire, and the flaming
lovers had returned. The fire-woman's head was tossed back
with my own, and her burning lover dripped her backward,
his featureless face buried between her breasts.

"Fire sprites," Tarove whispered as he pulled me towards
him again. "They're showing off, I think, for your benefit."

Then he was on me, hitching one of my bare legs over his
hip, his hands cupping my ass, and my nose filling with the
intoxicating honeysuckle scent of him. My dress had tattered,
and as he dipped me backward, it split up one thigh. Laughter
echoed around us as the drums became heavier, the natives
grinding around us, touching, entwined, their bodies moving
to the music fluidly. Tarove spun me slowly, his forehead
against my own. He pressed his hips closer, the bulge in his
pants obvious.

"I *will* kill you," I told him, unable to suppress a small
moan as he ground against me again.

He laughed heartily, and the delight on his face robbed me
of my breath for a moment. "You can try. I find the pro-
spect . . . exciting."

He spun me away, only to pull me back, and I stumbled,
nearly falling to my knees. He caught me by the waist, crushing me against him again. The dancers around us faded, and
I couldn't help but glance at the fiery apparitions beside us
again, their heat soaking the small of my back with sweat.

Fire Sprites.

I'd landed in the middle of a fairytale.

I moved away from Tarove, just out of his reach, running my hands down my chest, my hips. His eyes flashed a brilliant white, his lips parting.

God, what the hell was I doing?

Truthfully, I no longer cared.

One of the natives shimmied by and passed me something small, round, and orange. Fruit, by the looks of it. I saw Tarove's eyes widen in what appeared to be alarm, his mouth opened, and one arm outstretched in warning, but with a wicked snarl, I bit into the offering.

Deliciousness beyond anything I'd ever experienced flooded my mouth, and I moaned, swallowing the first bite as quickly as I could, suddenly ravenous. I went in for the second bite like a starving animal, but just before I could sink my teeth into the incredibly sweet flesh of the exotic manna, Tarove ripped it away, throwing it behind him with a snarl of frustration.

"If you thought the Gold was discomfiting, you're in for a rude awakening. This fruit is reserved for slaves—*sex slaves.* Another bite of that, and you'd be drooling on the sand, unable to remember your mother's name."

I laughed.

His hand shot out, grasped my hair, and tilted my head back, none-too-gently.

"You should evacuate it. Now." His jaw twitched. I'm guessing he wanted me to hurl.

The band around my ankle heated.

"I don't want to."

"I'm ordering you."

The lust from the tea had been light foreplay.

Need arched my back, overpowering the sting of the ankle band. The warmth immediately spread between my thighs, my nipples hardening.

I shivered at his hands on me, my hips squirming, my

whole body straining towards Tarove. He didn't release his hold on my hair, but his icy eyes swirled violet again, and his jaw clenched. His hair tickled my face, and I reached up, pinching a platinum lock between my fingers, rubbing it across my upper lip. I bit down on the lock, grinding it between my teeth.

"Please," I heard the raw desire in my voice, the hunger, and Tarove heard it, too.

"Please?" He questioned, his voice gravelly, alarmingly even.

For a split-second, I struggled to recall ever wanting Mitch this badly — ever wanting anything this badly — but I couldn't.

"*Please*," I repeated, harsher now, hating myself more than I ever had and needing his touch beyond measure. "Take me somewhere private. *Now*."

Chapter Nine: Forbidden Fruit

The band's heat cooled, but I hadn't even noticed the horrible tickle of the controlling ghost spiders until they crept away.

His smile was cold and mirthless, the violet in his eyes now an electric mix of stormy lightning and something else I couldn't read. He was breathing faster now, his grip on my hair tightening.

Then he was sweeping me off my feet.

My arms shot out, twining around his neck and tugging, wanting his mouth in places that should make me feel ashamed. His mouth was too far away, and I hissed through my teeth, nibbling at the flesh of his bicep, tracing one of his runes with my tongue. The purple flames with the ethereal lovers turned his hair a shade of violet, not unlike the shade of his pupils, creating shadows on his strong jaw, making him look more brutish, feral.

The hanging blue grass door of the hut was cool against the heat of my skin as it parted for us with a whisper, and I grasped for more of Tarove's flesh, sinking the nails of one hand into his shoulder blade. He released a long breath, shuddering against me, and I thrilled at the small victory. At shaking the beast.

He lowered me gently onto another braided mat. This one softer, larger, and smelled faintly of something minty. Flowers were hung, supple and fragrant and of shades that my human eyes had trouble labeling, their petals scattered about the floor. A small hearth sat in the corner, round and glowing orange from whatever fuel burned within.

I was pulling the dress over my head before he even low-ered himself to his knees, his trousers vanishing. He left be-hind snug, black boxers, his thick, muscled thighs straining the fabric.

And they weren't the only thing straining the fabric. I was apparently not alone in my excitement.

I writhed on the mat, my mind reeling with images of him behind me, below me, of sweat glistening on that perfect chest as he claimed me, over and over.

I'd lost my goddamn mind.

I was need and lust and pornographic dreams, and I was certain I would die if he couldn't deliver relief.

The fruit.

The damned fruit had obliterated everything I'd held dear with one bite, replacing softness, weakness, and rage with a narrow vision that focused solely on the specimen tugging away my panties, and god, did it ever feel wonderful. The pri-mal savagery of throwing it all to the wind, of replacing my thoughts and dreams and grief with cold, hard lust.

He was sexuality incarnate. Large, golden hands smoothed over my outer thighs, his eyes glowed, never leaving mine. His touch was more powerful than any chemical I'd con-sumed so far, and I released the breath I hadn't realized I'd been holding. I bucked, needing his fingers closer to where I ached, dripping wet. I spread my legs wider in anticipation, my hands going to my breasts.

His eyes, fiery with passion, took me in. He growled deep in his throat, his gaze working from my breasts, then to my neck, only to linger on my mouth. When he met my eyes, his own softened, something strangely akin to pity slackening his mouth.

Then he froze.

Gone was the lightning in his spectacular eyes. His mouth snapped shut as he tensed, pushing away from my impatient body roughly.

I could have wept and nearly did, making a choked sound of disappointment.

"Wha—" I began.

He tossed my clothing back to me, which hit me rudely in the face. I was suddenly aware of the drums outside again, their seductive, heady beat mocking.

My blood cooled.

There wasn't a drug on earth or beyond that could fuck a woman up so badly that she couldn't feel the bite of rejection.

My fuzzy, thirsty thoughts fled with such speed that it rocked me, and I let my head drop back onto the mat, uncaring that the thud hurt, and I welcomed the pain.

My nakedness was now an object of total and complete shame, and I pushed myself onto my ass, struggling with the flimsy fabric, unable to find the opening and cursing the she-devils that had worked me into it.

Tarove stood, having evidently used his clothing-magic to replace his missing suit. He now wore a plain white tee and tight, black jeans. Black boots were laced to his knees, silver buckles gleaming. He belonged on the cover of a new-age romance novel, posed with a sword, demons gathered behind him.

I vehemently wished that I had a sword, but as to whether I'd use it on myself or him, I didn't know.

One of us would have a bellyache, that's for sure.

"Drugged again." I spat.

"Drugged? As if you were force-fed the *Aspladahe*. If you recall, I tried to prevent the consumption."

"I was hoping it would kill me!"

"You lie. You felt reckless, human. You were, what is the word? *Horny*. Like the female in your holy book, you saw forbidden fruit, and you chose to taste it."

"I'd like for you to taste my fist in your—" I was cut off

with searing agony as the band around my ankle heated to a temperature that I'd only experienced at the whim of the good doctor back at the auction. Molten pain spread across my scalp, and a million tiny hornets inserted their hypodermic needles into my spine all the way to my tailbone. My legs stiffened, toes pointing outwards. My fingers curled into talons, and I felt the remainder of my manicure snapping on my palms.

Then it was over. Bloody tears leaked from my eyes, and I wiped them away angrily, my breath coming in between hitching sobs.

"Do not forget who is in control here, pet."

I was dragged unceremoniously to my feet and ordered to put the dress on with haste. Tarove watched me fumble desperately, a sadistic smile turning his beauty cruel as he took obvious pleasure in my clumsy hands.

I ached to strike him. To pummel him with my fists until his perfection was mush, but with the memory of the pain he'd just inflicted fresh, I didn't have the balls to do so. Instead, I settled for channeling all my hate into my glare, and I hoped that it irked him, this one small defiance.

Oh God. I'd nearly given myself to him. No, I'd *flung* myself at him. This monster that'd purchased me with the nonchalance of a farmer buying a sow to fatten for the upcoming winter months. He and his kind had violated my womb, manipulated my desires, and taken me away from the only true love I'd ever known.

Mitch.

I'd forgotten my love so easily, and the small band that hadn't been present when I'd woke to learn that the world as I'd known it was no more. I wondered if the nurse had plucked the ring from my finger and tossed it into the trash. I wondered if she'd sneered at its lack of luster, so surrounded were they by so much indulgence, though to me, it'd been fit for a princess.

A couple of shots of libido tea and a bite of orgasmic fruit, and I'd been reduced to little more than a groveling bitch in heat, clawing at Tarove's neck as if he weren't going to kill me once he'd gotten a taste of strange.

My nostrils flared with rage, the last of the heat left. My body tensed, not with drugged desire, but with the burning need to hurl itself violently at the beautiful devil watching me, absently stroking his chin as if he'd not been ravenous for me only a few moments prior.

"This band," I spat, as I struggled to zip what remained of the dress in the back. "It's not unlike a cattle prod, is it? Does it come with an instruction manual? Can you buy it at your local markets? Do you have a button?"

"It's infused with our blood, bound to our will, and can never, ever be removed." He smiled, eyes glowing briefly like a Halloween pumpkin.

A wave of dizziness hit me then, and I staggered, wrenching my arm away when his hand shot out to steady me. He released me as if my flesh had burned his palm, lips turning down at the corners, and when he cupped the back of my neck, his fingers spasmed, as if he longed to squeeze until my head separated from my body.

"Reprieve is over. We're going home."

"Not *my* home." I stumbled as he pushed my face through the hanging blue grass. "It will never be *my* home."

"We're sifting this time. I'm fairly certain you've been exposed to enough *Other* to withstand it without your atoms scattering about the universe. If you don't survive, please accept my insincere apologies in advance."

"Sifting?" I asked, and before I could mull the strange word over, he'd pulled me close.

"The tunnels were for your benefit, but I no longer care what benefits you."

His mouth crushed against mine, tongue pushing between

my lips, and a disorienting orgy of colors burst behind my eyes. I saw men on sleek black horses, their white hair flying behind them, bows raised, and swords unsheathed, heads dipped low as they pounded through a dead forest. I saw the birth of planets, a black hole devouring the triple suns, and a woman being gutted by her lover in a bed as large as my house back home. I saw creatures with seven mouths climbing rocky cliffs, only to be split into by the steel of Tarove's sword. I saw him crushing enemies by his will alone, their eyes bursting in their sockets, their mouths leaking fat rivers of blood as they begged for a quicker end.

I felt pleasure, orgasmic, so intense that I wanted to be split down the center by his blade because I knew that it would tear me apart.

I'd had no idea what I'd been teasing, baiting.

As I crumpled in his arms, I wondered if I would ever recover from whatever he'd just done to my simple, human mind. No one from my world could ever begin to comprehend them—the Faye. We were so far down the food chain that I wondered why they even allowed our kind to exist. How insulting it must be to contain the secrets of the universe and the knowledge to bend it at your will and walk among cocky beings that thought they were nearly your equal. Why did they bother to bargain with us? Why did they not rape and conquer? It would be easy. Oh-so-easy for them.

We blipped out, leaving the beach behind, and I traveled through the cosmos, my soul breaking apart and trailing behind me. I imagined that my body turned inside out, my organs exposed to the meteors and stardust. I became a mote of dust, tumbling from the rough exhalation of a giant, bathed in the fire of a world comprised entirely of lava and bone and blackened, screaming faces.

I was nothing.

When the travel stopped, I couldn't focus on the glittering

courtyard around us, nor could I understand what the smooth, sensual voices around me were saying. My nose was assaulted by dozens of unfamiliar scents, each just as delicious as the other, and there wasn't a part on my body, or within it, that wasn't raw.

Tarove's arms might have been salt, large grains of it, rubbing cruelly into my wounds.

"We're home," he whispered. "You're going to live. You will come to me again, and by choice, and then, and only then, will I claim you. Look around, Kelly Mayking. Welcome to Faerie."

About the Author

I became involved with romance quite by accident. My fourth novel, Straight from the Heart, was literally a novel idea of mine that turned out to gain high praise. I never intended to write romance, but it's my strength. This story is a mix. Enjoy.

www.ingramcontent.com/pod-product-compliance
Lightning Source LLC
Chambersburg PA
CBHW070224140626
46555CB00018B/1273